ATOS Book Level: 2.8
AR Points: 0.5
Quiz #: 140122 [X] RP [ ] LS [ ] VP
Lexile: 480

# GHOSTLY GRAPHIC ADVENTURES

# THE SPOOKY SHORT SANDS SHIPWRECK

Written by Baron Specter
Illustrated by Dustin Evans

magic wagon

visit us at www.abdopublishing.com

Published by Magic Wagon, a division of the ABDO Group, 8000 West 78th Street, Edina, Minnesota 55439. Copyright © 2011 by Abdo Consulting Group, Inc. International copyrights reserved in all countries. All rights reserved. No part of this book may be reproduced in any form without written permission from the publisher.

Graphic Planet™ is a trademark and logo of Magic Wagon.

Printed in the United States of America, North Mankato, Minnesota.
042010
092010
♻ This book contains at least 10% recycled materials.

Written by Baron Specter
Illustrated by Dustin Evans
Lettered and designed by Ardden Entertainment LLC
Edited by Stephanie Hedlund and Rochelle Baltzer
Cover art by Dustin Evans
Cover design by Ardden Entertainment LLC

**Library of Congress Cataloging-in-Publication Data**

Specter, Baron, 1957-
  The fourth adventure : the spooky Short Sands shipwreck / by Baron Specter ; illustrated by Dustin Evans.
       p. cm. -- (Ghostly graphic adventures)
  Summary: While on vacation in Maine, Joey, Tank, and Gill explore an 18th century shipwreck that is uncovered by a storm and soon find themselves part of its ghostly crew.
  ISBN 978-1-60270-773-3
  1. Graphic novels. [1. Graphic novels. 2. Ghosts--Fiction. 3. Time travel--Fiction. 4. Shipwrecks--Fiction. 5. Seafaring life--Fiction. 6. Maine--Fiction.] I. Evans, Dustin, 1982- ill. II. Title. III. Title: Spooky Short Sands shipwreck.
  PZ7.7.S648Fou 2010
  741.5'973--dc22
                                    2009052893

# TABLE OF CONTENTS

Our Heroes and Villains ...................... 4

The Spooky Short Sands Shipwreck.......... 5

The Short Sands Shipwreck .................. 31

Glossary ................................. 32

Web Sites................................. 32

# OUR HEROES AND VILLAINS

## Joey DeAngelo
Hero

## The Captain
Villain

## Gil
Hero

## The First Mate
Villain

## Tank
Hero

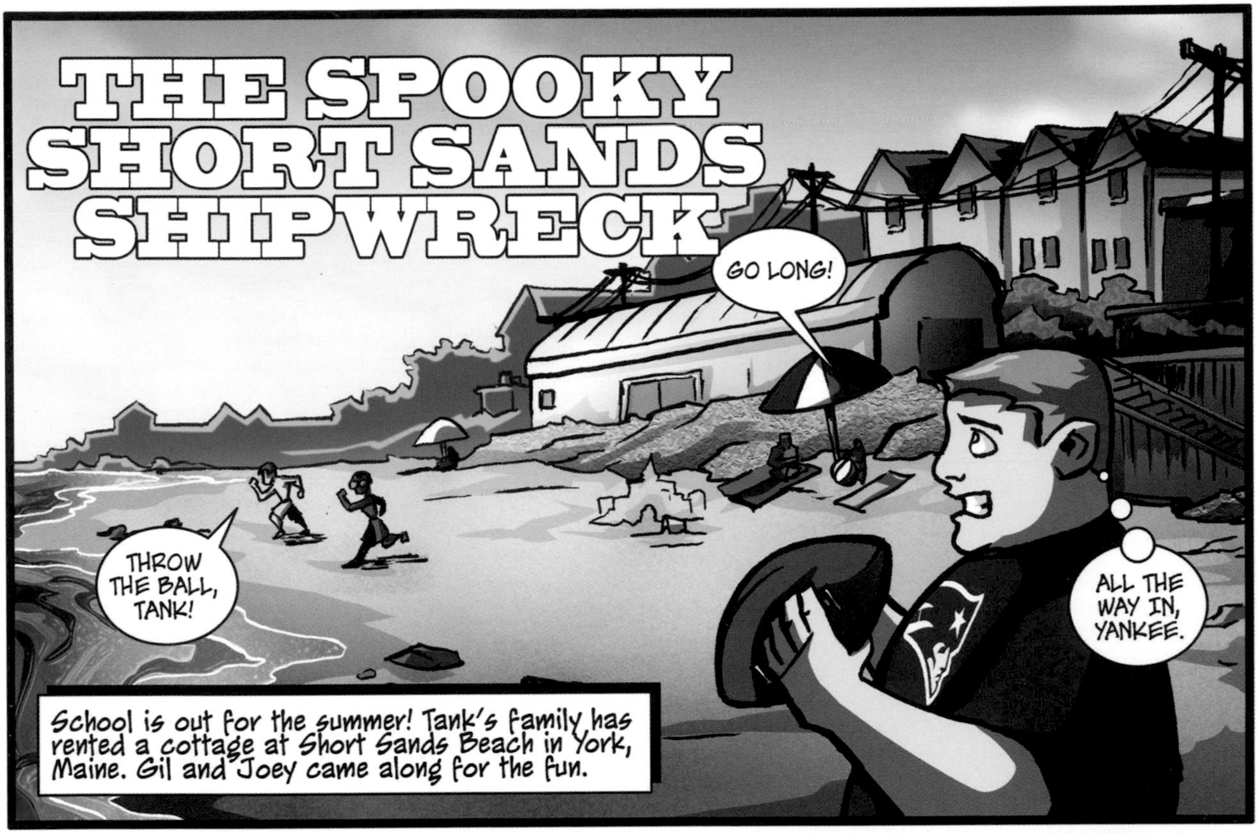
THE SPOOKY SHORT SANDS SHIPWRECK
THROW THE BALL, TANK!
GO LONG!
ALL THE WAY IN, YANKEE.
School is out for the summer! Tank's family has rented a cottage at Short Sands Beach in York, Maine. Gil and Joey came along for the fun.

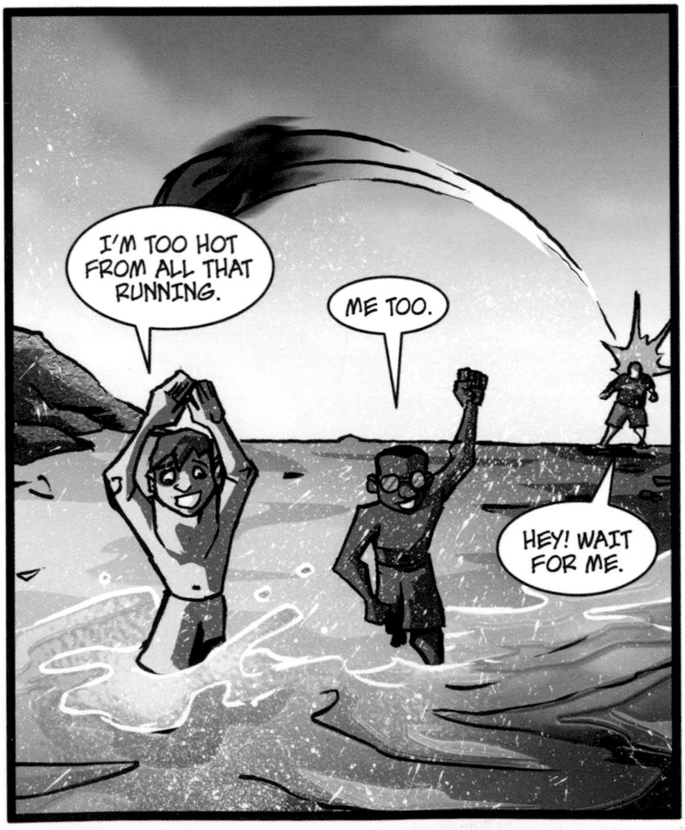
I'M TOO HOT FROM ALL THAT RUNNING.
ME TOO.
HEY! WAIT FOR ME.

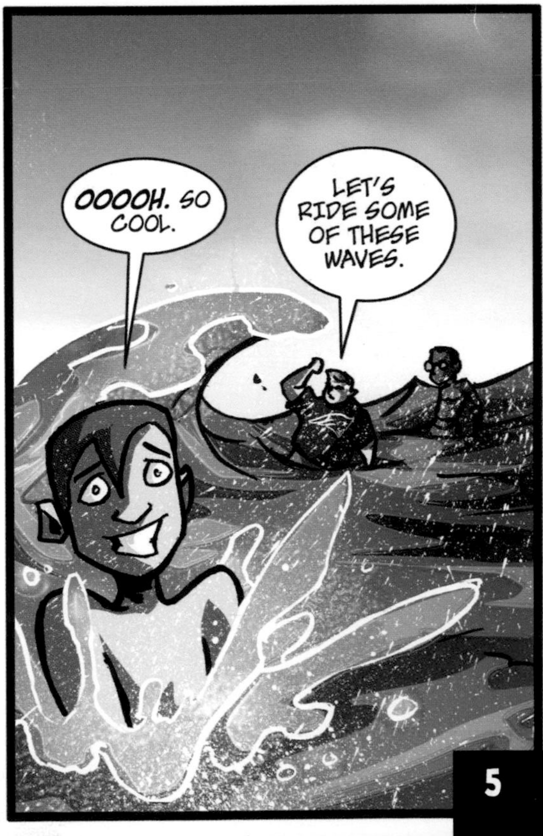
OOOOH. SO COOL.
LET'S RIDE SOME OF THESE WAVES.

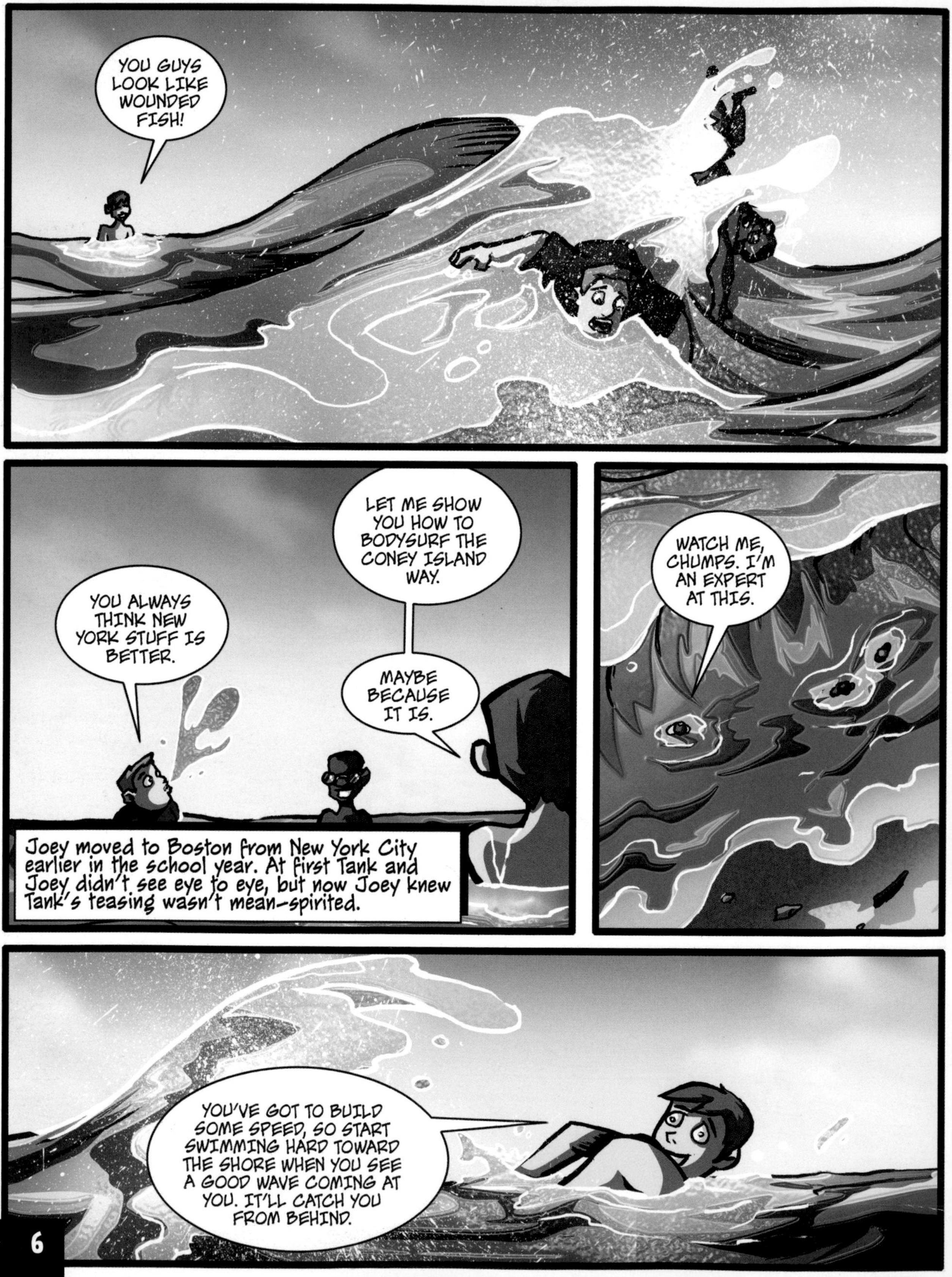
YOU GUYS LOOK LIKE WOUNDED FISH!
YOU ALWAYS THINK NEW YORK STUFF IS BETTER.
LET ME SHOW YOU HOW TO BODYSURF THE CONEY ISLAND WAY.
MAYBE BECAUSE IT IS.
Joey moved to Boston from New York City earlier in the school year. At first Tank and Joey didn't see eye to eye, but now Joey knew Tank's teasing wasn't mean-spirited.
WATCH ME, CHUMPS. I'M AN EXPERT AT THIS.
YOU'VE GOT TO BUILD SOME SPEED, SO START SWIMMING HARD TOWARD THE SHORE WHEN YOU SEE A GOOD WAVE COMING AT YOU. IT'LL CATCH YOU FROM BEHIND.

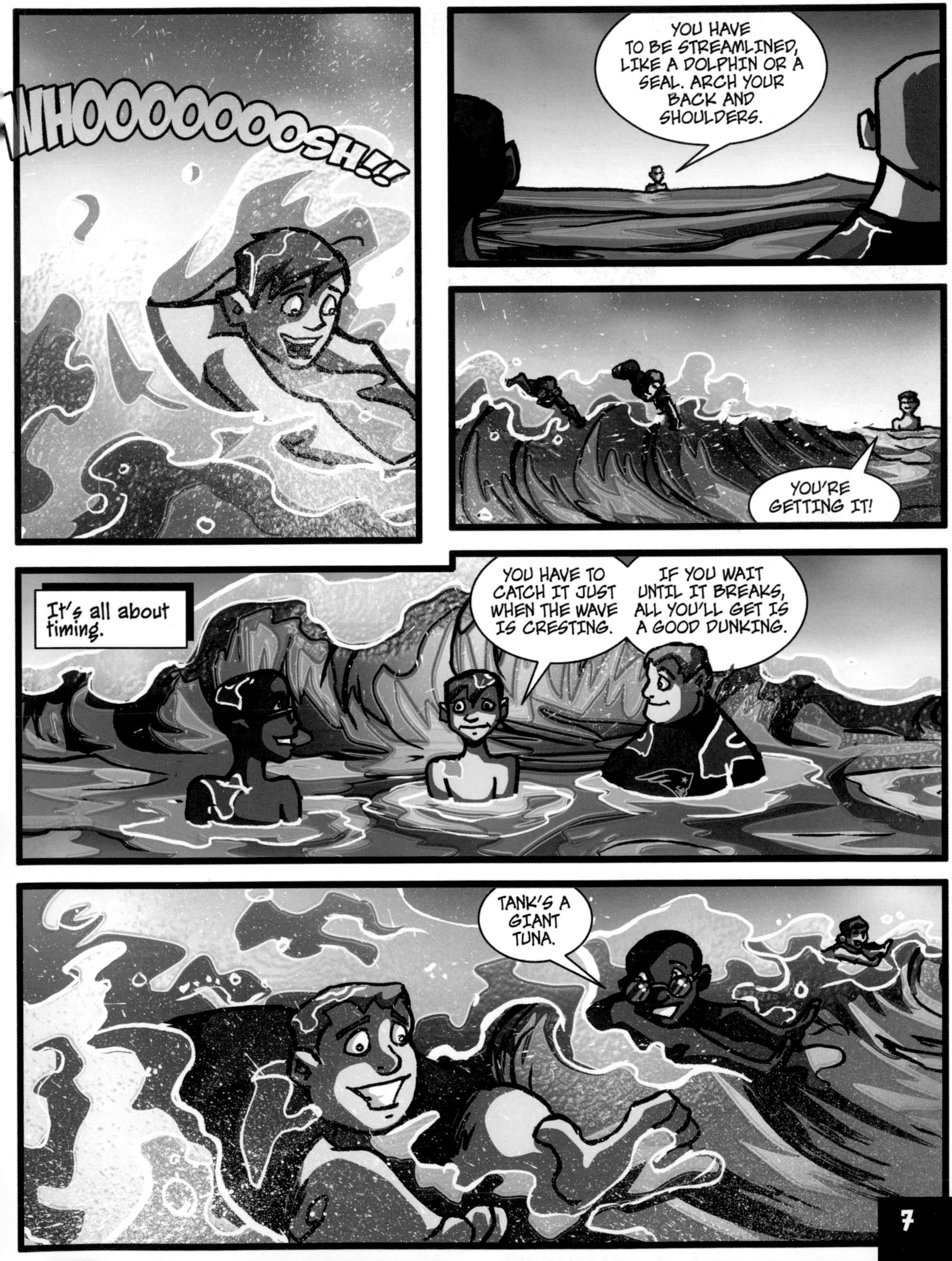
WHOOOOOOOSH!!!
YOU HAVE TO BE STREAMLINED, LIKE A DOLPHIN OR A SEAL. ARCH YOUR BACK AND SHOULDERS.
YOU'RE GETTING IT!
It's all about timing.
YOU HAVE TO CATCH IT JUST WHEN THE WAVE IS CRESTING.
IF YOU WAIT UNTIL IT BREAKS, ALL YOU'LL GET IS A GOOD DUNKING.
TANK'S A GIANT TUNA.

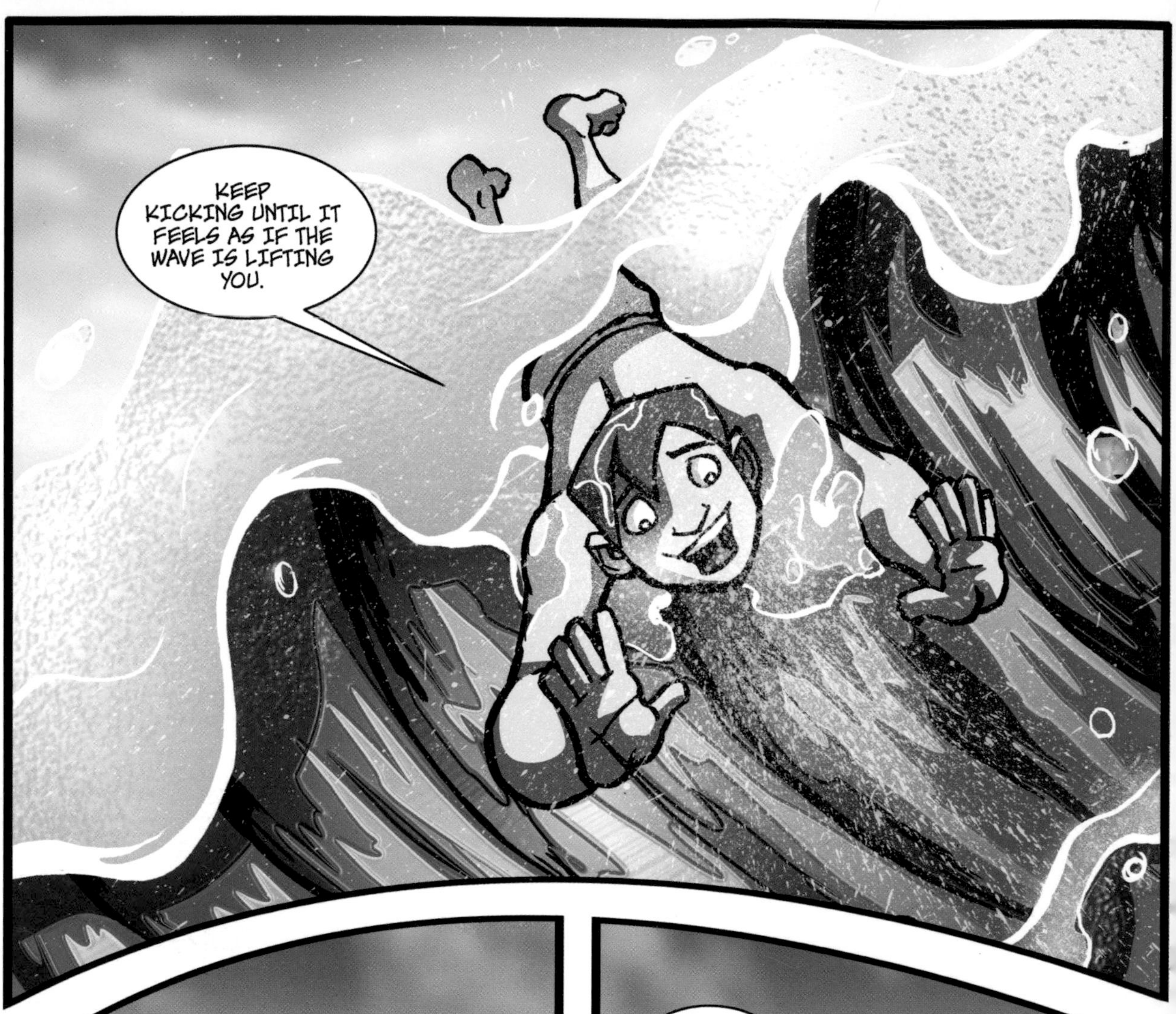
KEEP KICKING UNTIL IT FEELS AS IF THE WAVE IS LIFTING YOU.

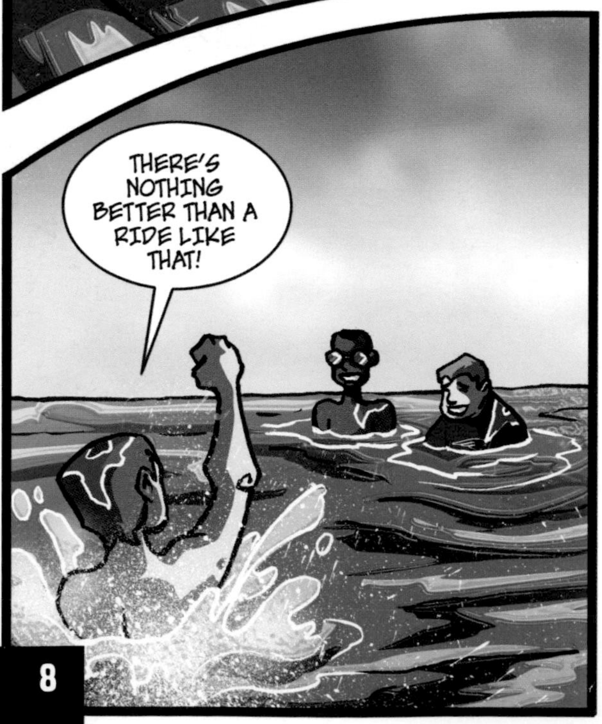
THERE'S NOTHING BETTER THAN A RIDE LIKE THAT!

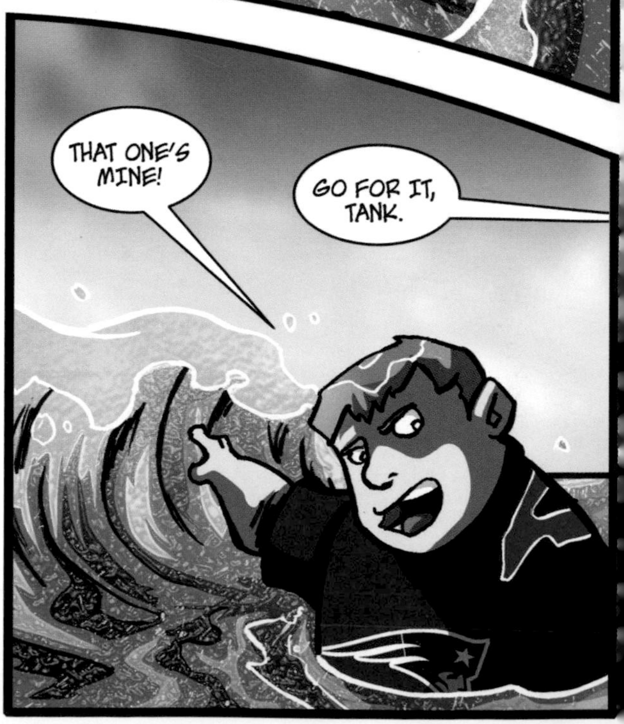
THAT ONE'S MINE!
GO FOR IT, TANK.

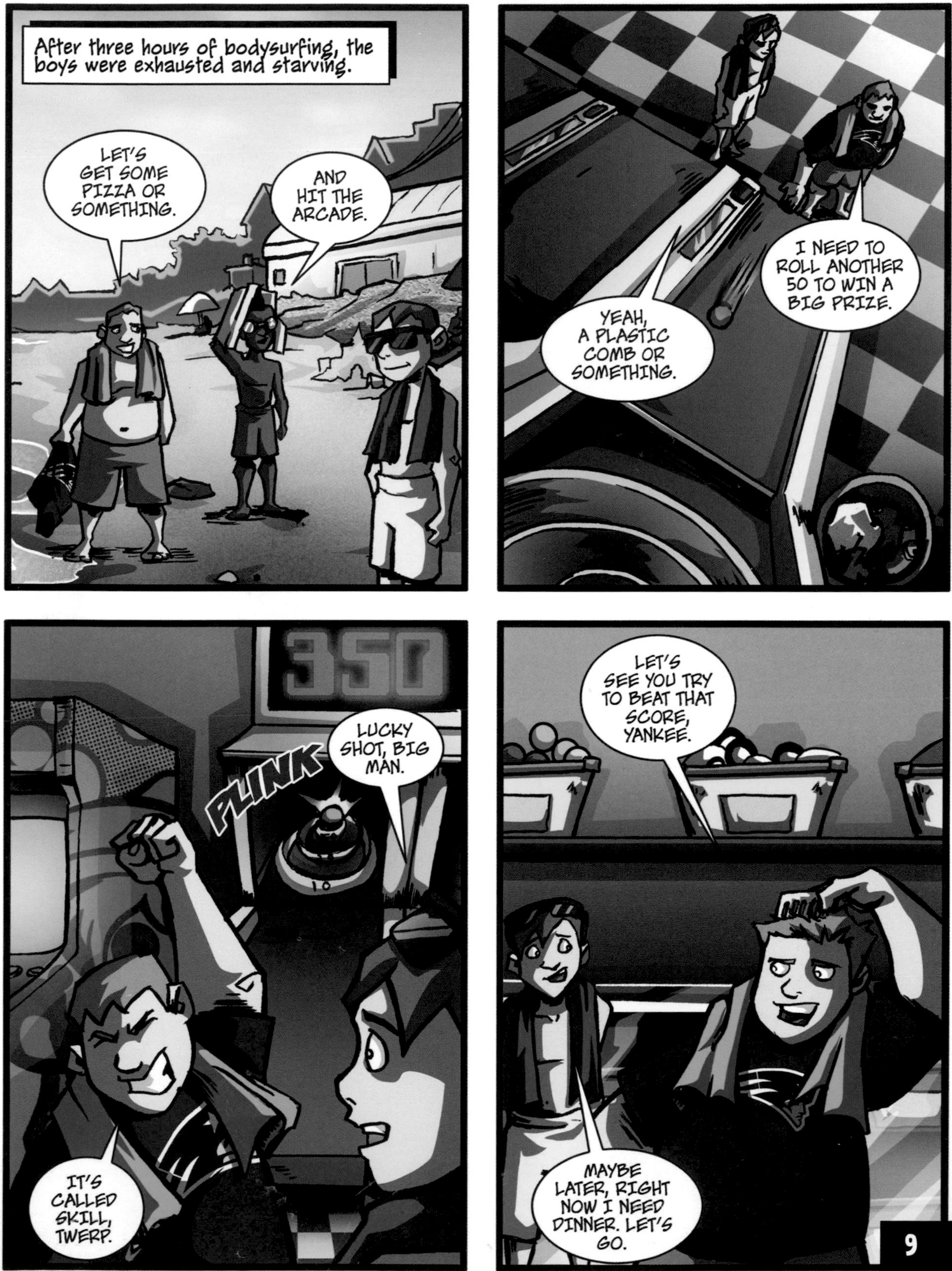

After three hours of bodysurfing, the boys were exhausted and starving.
LET'S GET SOME PIZZA OR SOMETHING.
AND HIT THE ARCADE.
I NEED TO ROLL ANOTHER 50 TO WIN A BIG PRIZE.
YEAH, A PLASTIC COMB OR SOMETHING.
350
PLINK
LUCKY SHOT, BIG MAN.
IT'S CALLED SKILL, TWERP.
LET'S SEE YOU TRY TO BEAT THAT SCORE, YANKEE.
MAYBE LATER, RIGHT NOW I NEED DINNER. LET'S GO.

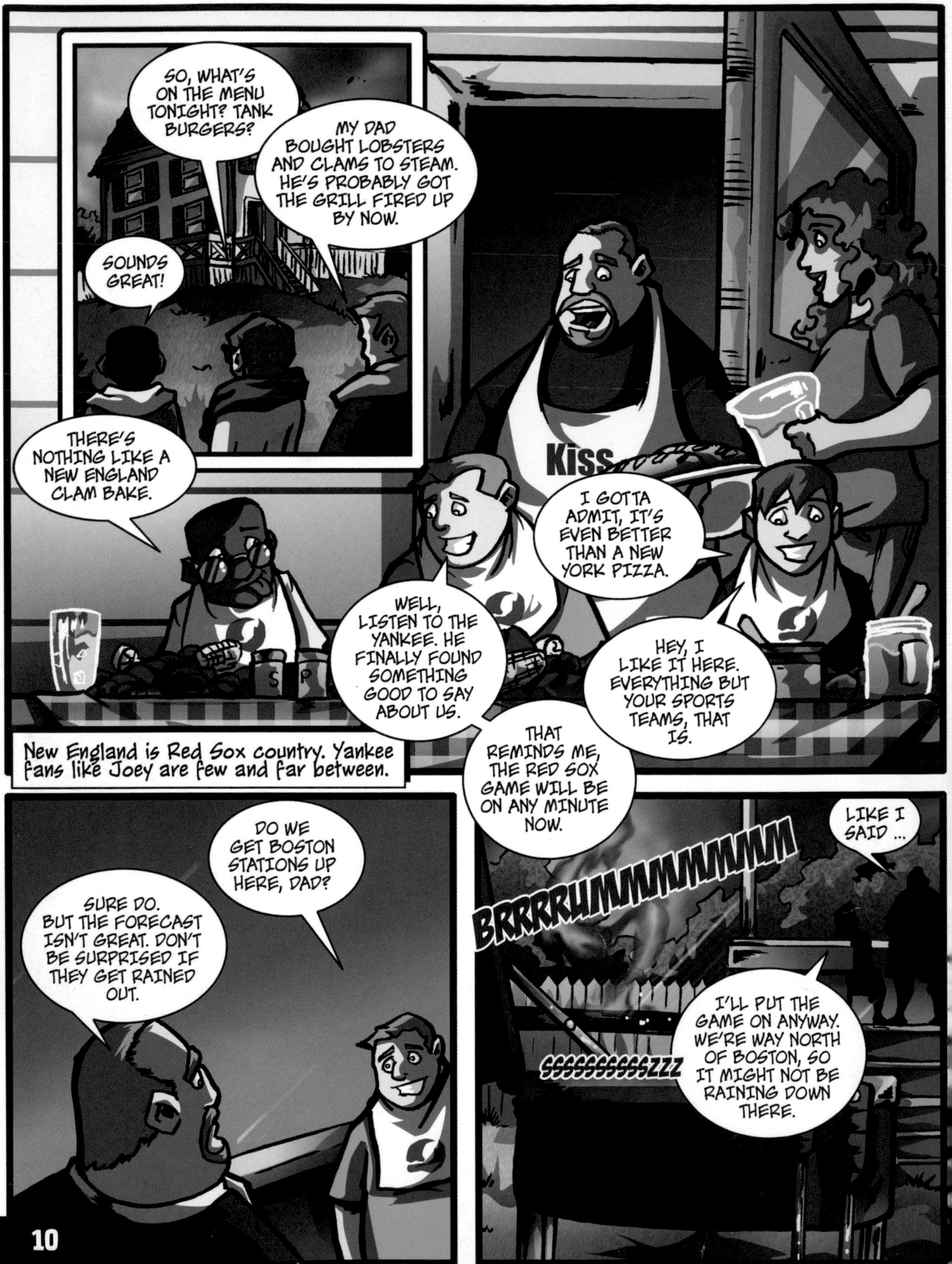
SO, WHAT'S ON THE MENU TONIGHT? TANK BURGERS?
MY DAD BOUGHT LOBSTERS AND CLAMS TO STEAM. HE'S PROBABLY GOT THE GRILL FIRED UP BY NOW.
SOUNDS GREAT!
Kiss
THERE'S NOTHING LIKE A NEW ENGLAND CLAM BAKE.
I GOTTA ADMIT, IT'S EVEN BETTER THAN A NEW YORK PIZZA.
WELL, LISTEN TO THE YANKEE. HE FINALLY FOUND SOMETHING GOOD TO SAY ABOUT US.
HEY, I LIKE IT HERE. EVERYTHING BUT YOUR SPORTS TEAMS, THAT IS.
New England is Red Sox country. Yankee fans like Joey are few and far between.
THAT REMINDS ME, THE RED SOX GAME WILL BE ON ANY MINUTE NOW.
DO WE GET BOSTON STATIONS UP HERE, DAD?
SURE DO. BUT THE FORECAST ISN'T GREAT. DON'T BE SURPRISED IF THEY GET RAINED OUT.
BRRRRUMMMMMMMMM
LIKE I SAID ...
SSSSSSSSSSZZZ
I'LL PUT THE GAME ON ANYWAY. WE'RE WAY NORTH OF BOSTON, SO IT MIGHT NOT BE RAINING DOWN THERE.

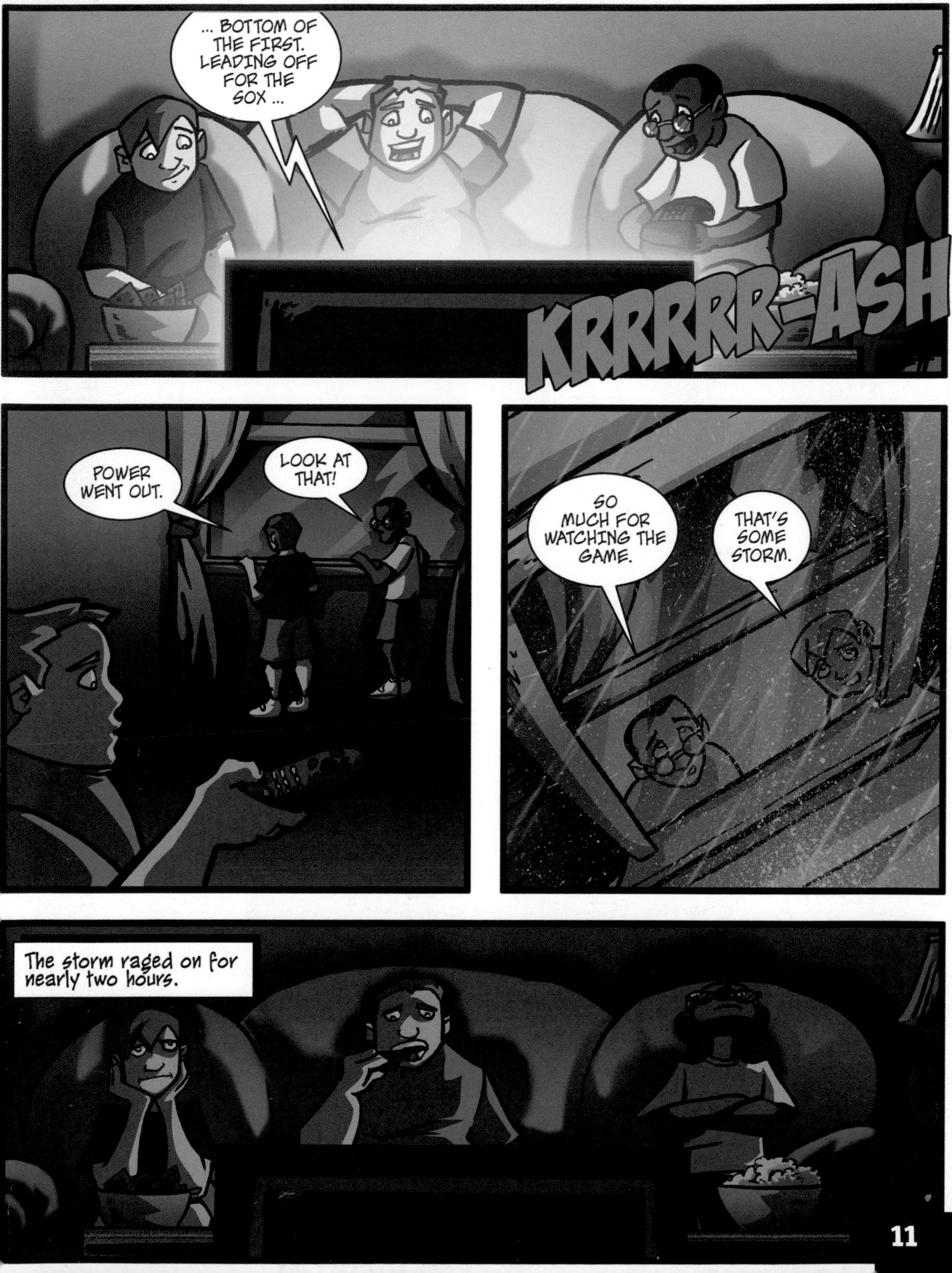
... BOTTOM OF THE FIRST. LEADING OFF FOR THE SOX ...
KRRRRR-ASH
POWER WENT OUT.
LOOK AT THAT!
SO MUCH FOR WATCHING THE GAME.
THAT'S SOME STORM.
The storm raged on for nearly two hours.

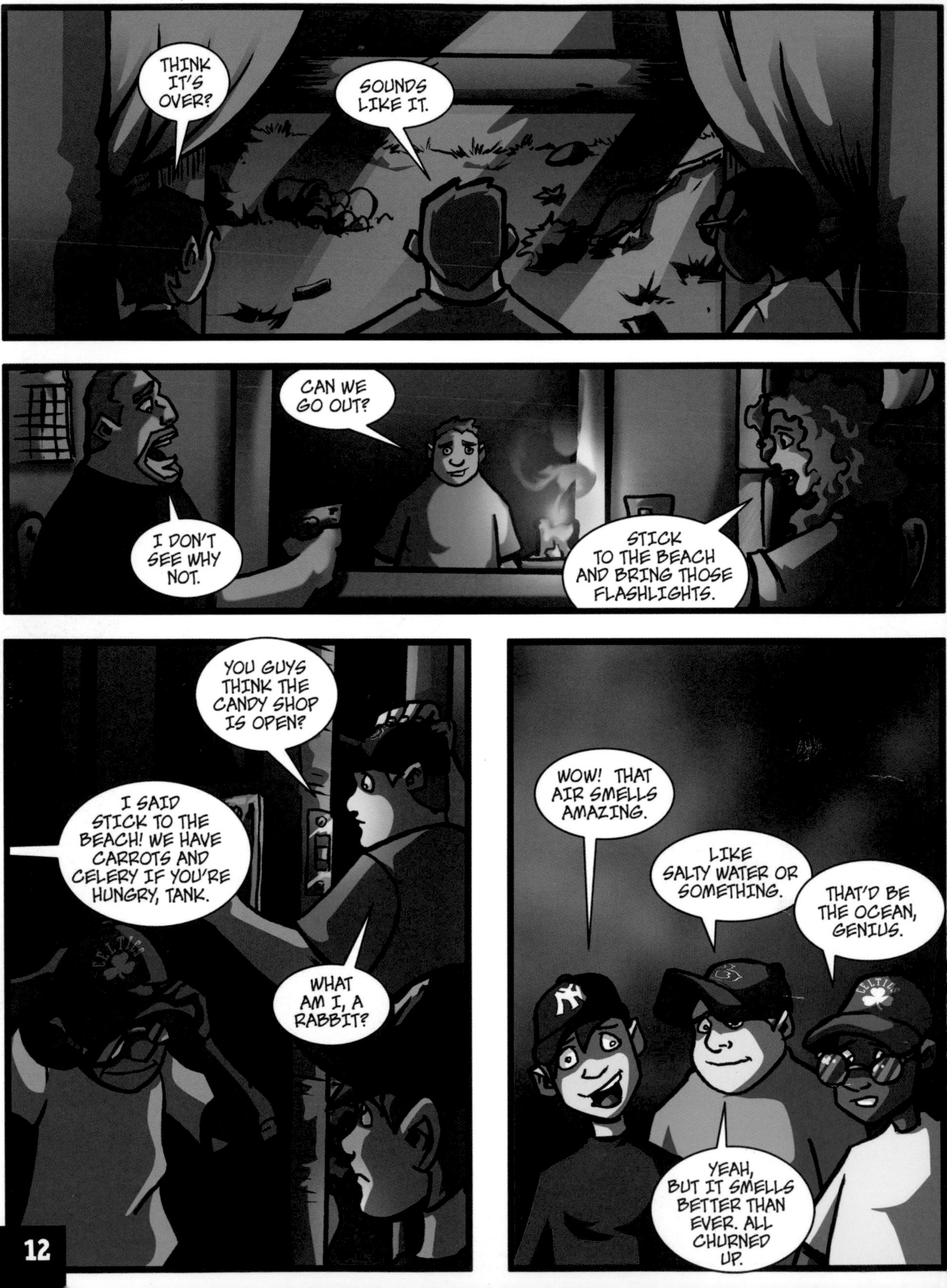
THINK IT'S OVER?
SOUNDS LIKE IT.
CAN WE GO OUT?
I DON'T SEE WHY NOT.
STICK TO THE BEACH AND BRING THOSE FLASHLIGHTS.
YOU GUYS THINK THE CANDY SHOP IS OPEN?
I SAID STICK TO THE BEACH! WE HAVE CARROTS AND CELERY IF YOU'RE HUNGRY, TANK.
WHAT AM I, A RABBIT?
WOW! THAT AIR SMELLS AMAZING.
LIKE SALTY WATER OR SOMETHING.
THAT'D BE THE OCEAN, GENIUS.
YEAH, BUT IT SMELLS BETTER THAN EVER. ALL CHURNED UP.

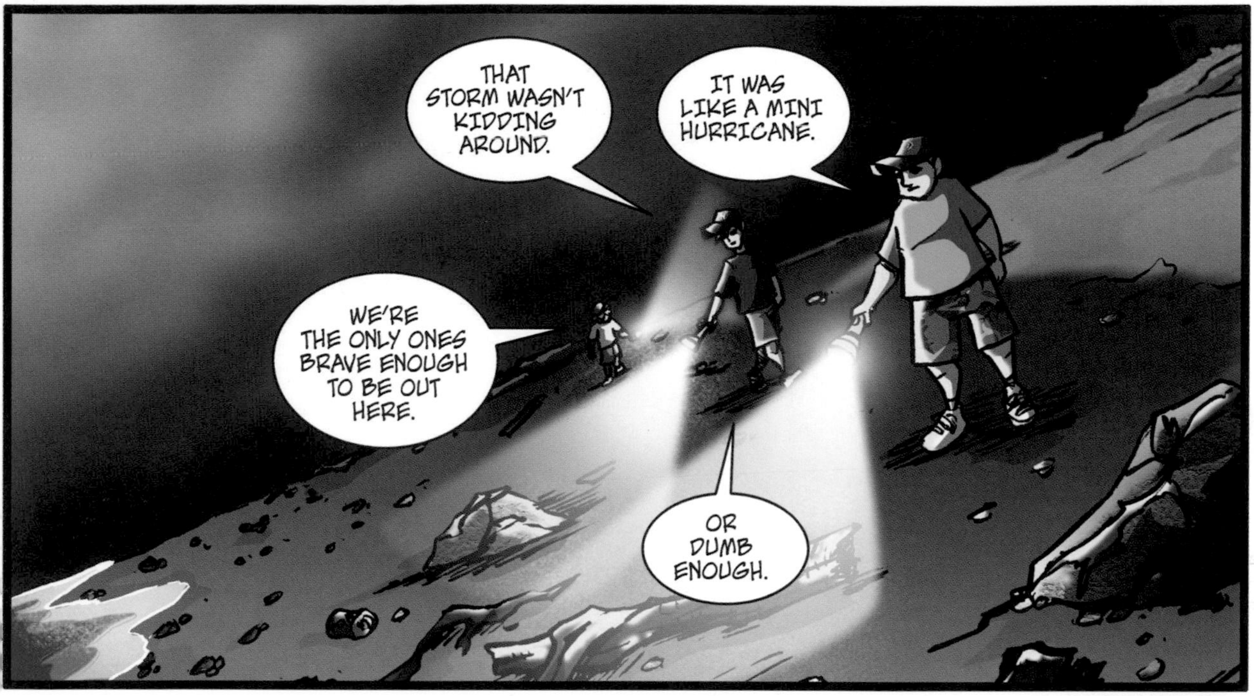
THAT STORM WASN'T KIDDING AROUND.
IT WAS LIKE A MINI HURRICANE.
WE'RE THE ONLY ONES BRAVE ENOUGH TO BE OUT HERE.
OR DUMB ENOUGH.

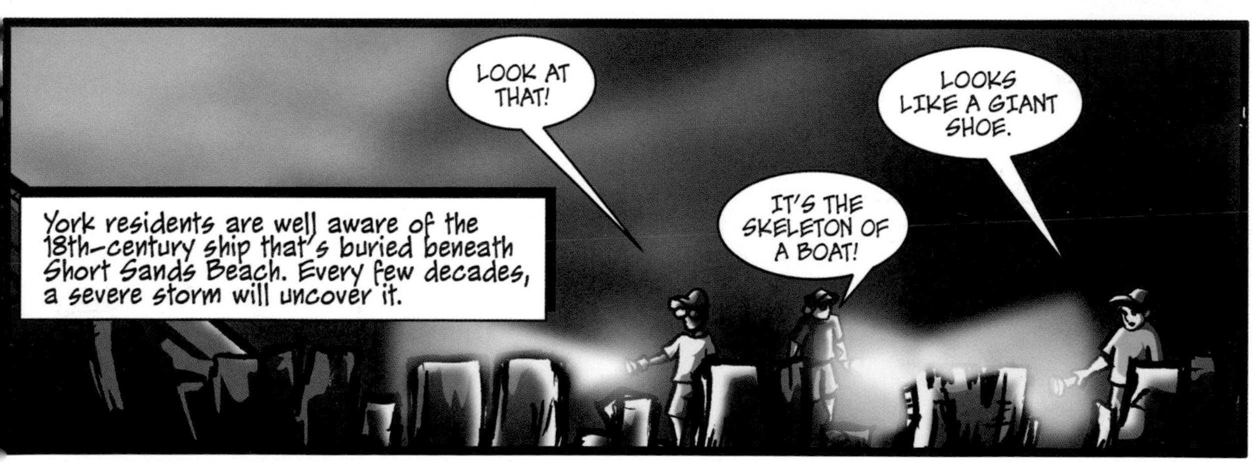
York residents are well aware of the 18th-century ship that's buried beneath Short Sands Beach. Every few decades, a severe storm will uncover it.
LOOK AT THAT!
LOOKS LIKE A GIANT SHOE.
IT'S THE SKELETON OF A BOAT!

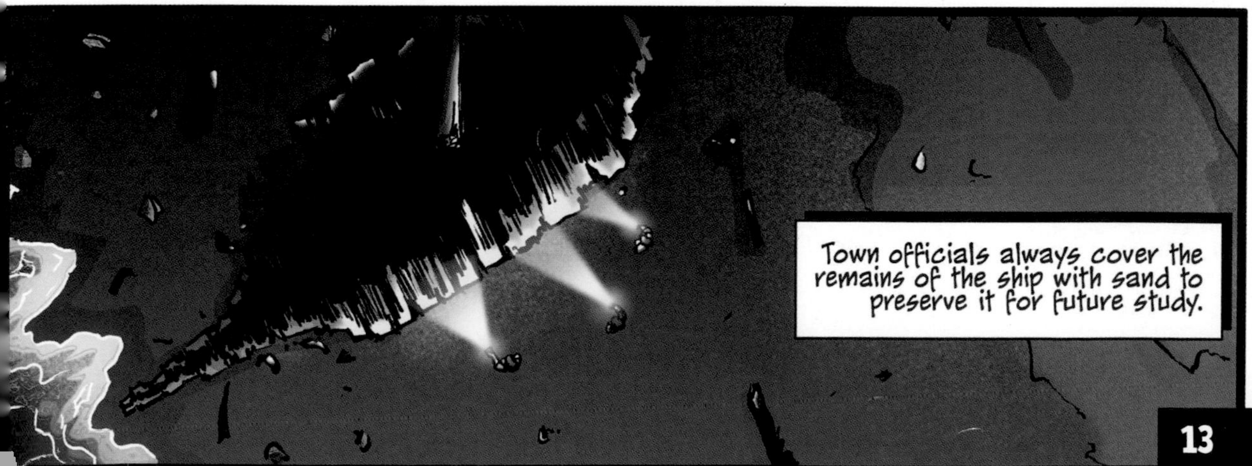
Town officials always cover the remains of the ship with sand to preserve it for future study.

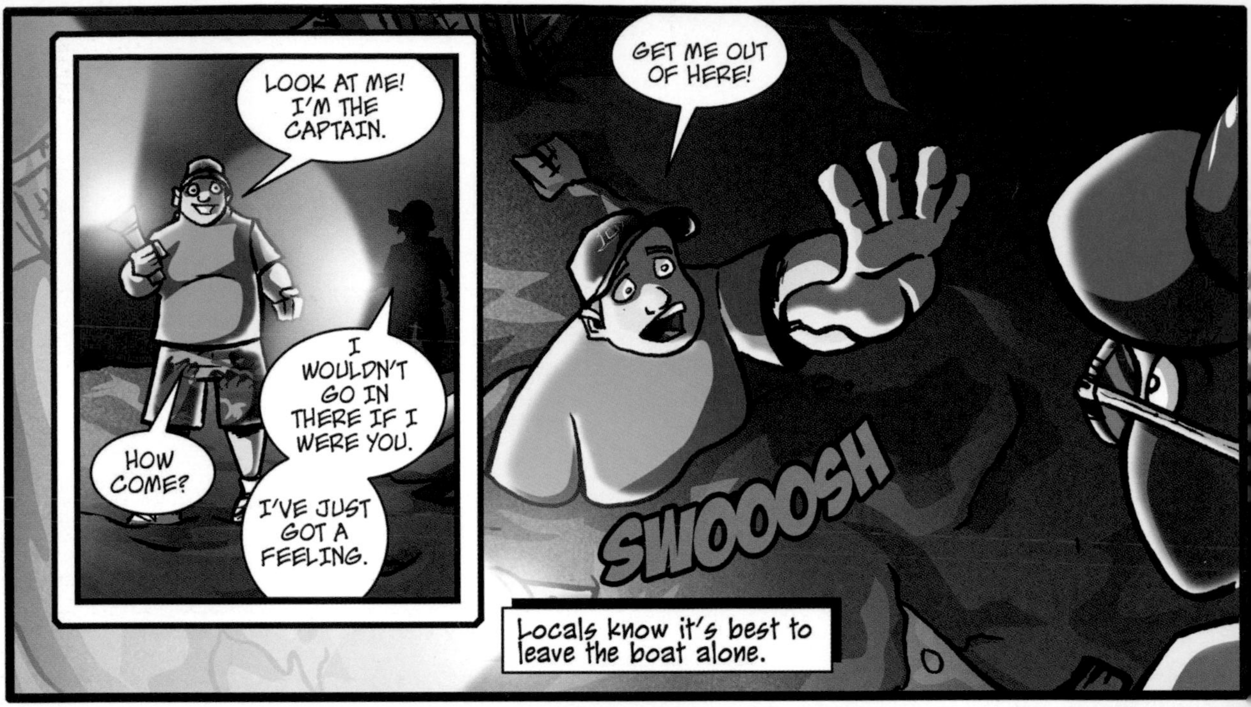
LOOK AT ME! I'M THE CAPTAIN.
I WOULDN'T GO IN THERE IF I WERE YOU.
HOW COME?
I'VE JUST GOT A FEELING.
GET ME OUT OF HERE!
SWOOOSH
Locals know it's best to leave the boat alone.

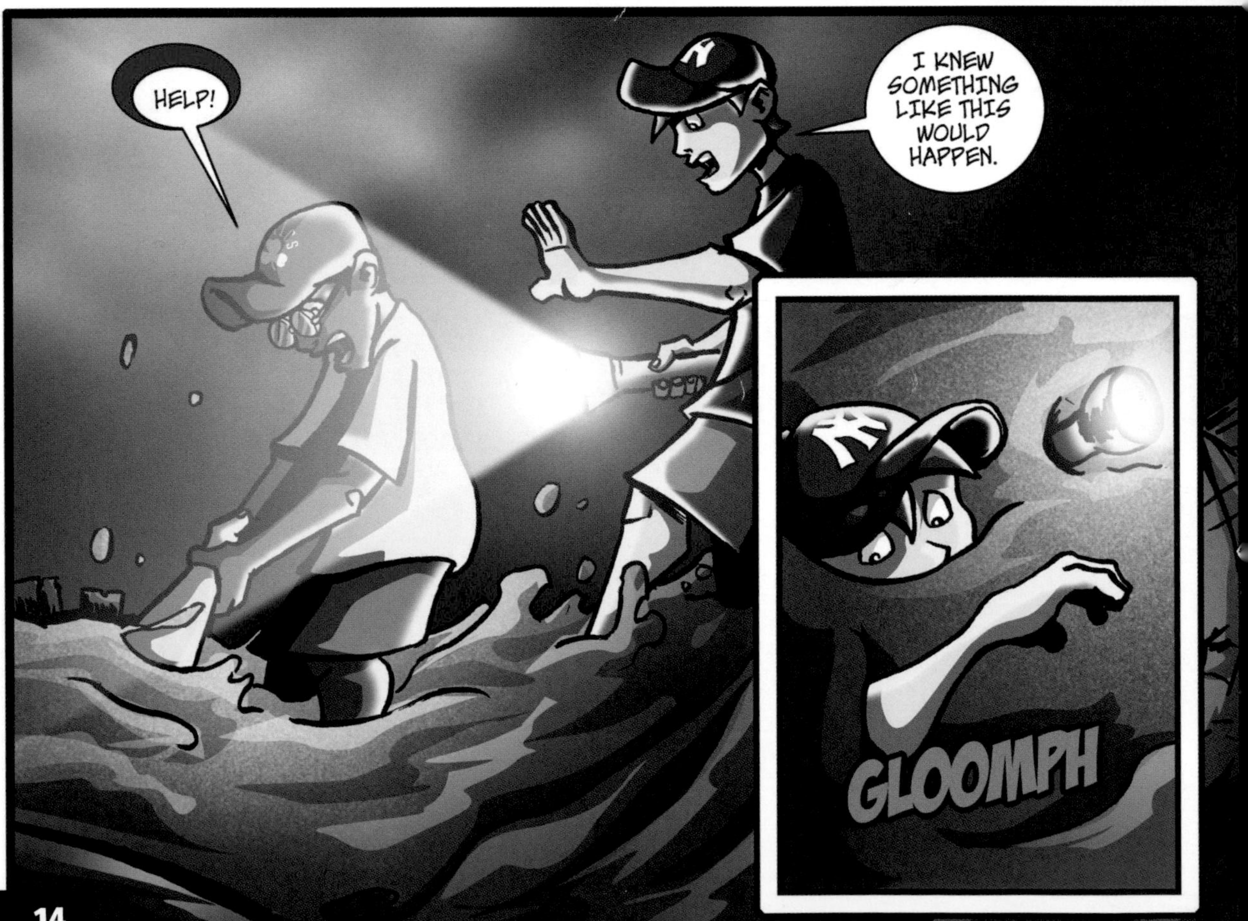
HELP!
I KNEW SOMETHING LIKE THIS WOULD HAPPEN.
GLOOMPH

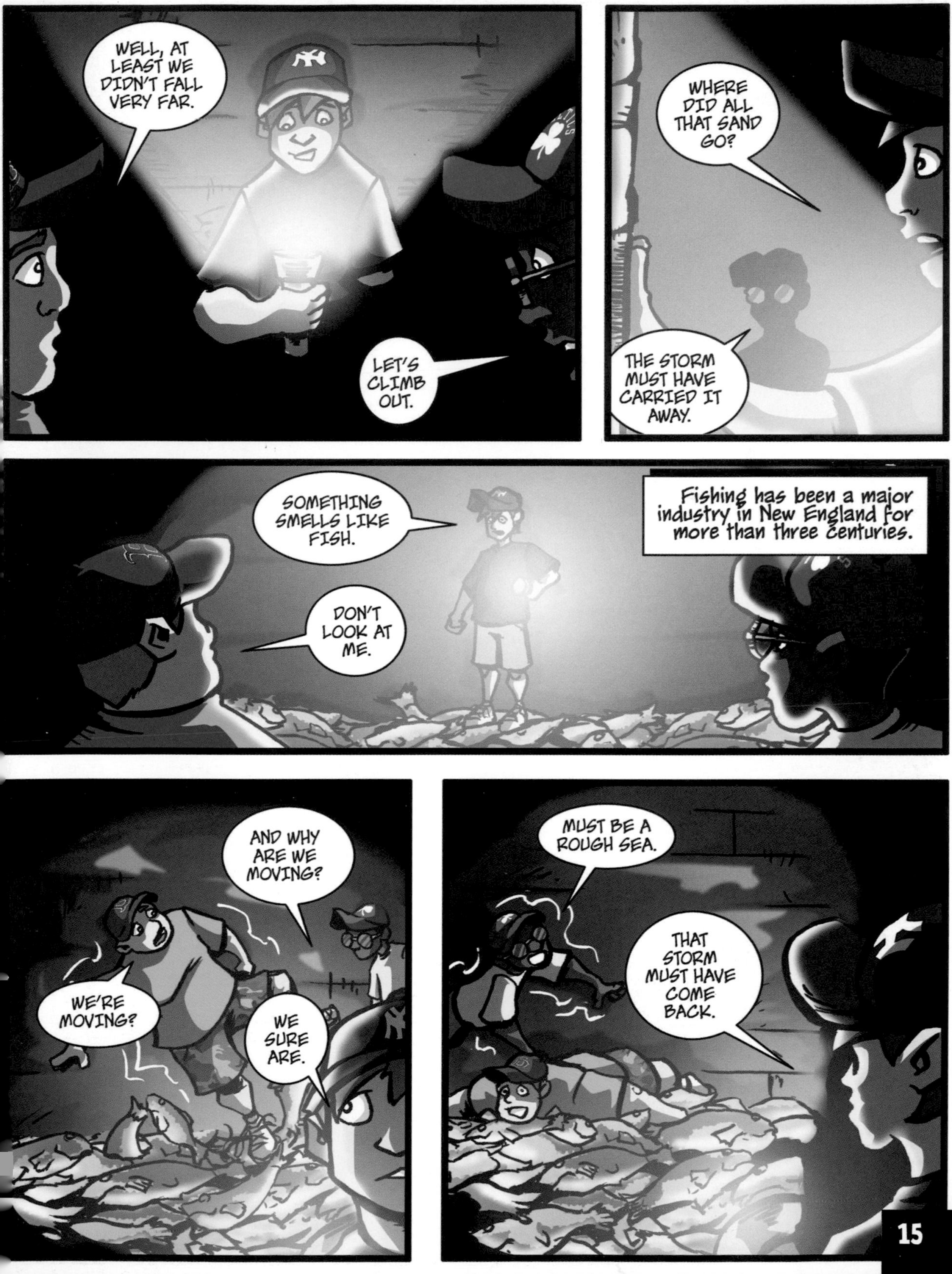
WELL, AT LEAST WE DIDN'T FALL VERY FAR.
LET'S CLIMB OUT.
WHERE DID ALL THAT SAND GO?
THE STORM MUST HAVE CARRIED IT AWAY.
Fishing has been a major industry in New England for more than three centuries.
SOMETHING SMELLS LIKE FISH.
DON'T LOOK AT ME.
AND WHY ARE WE MOVING?
WE'RE MOVING?
WE SURE ARE.
MUST BE A ROUGH SEA.
THAT STORM MUST HAVE COME BACK.

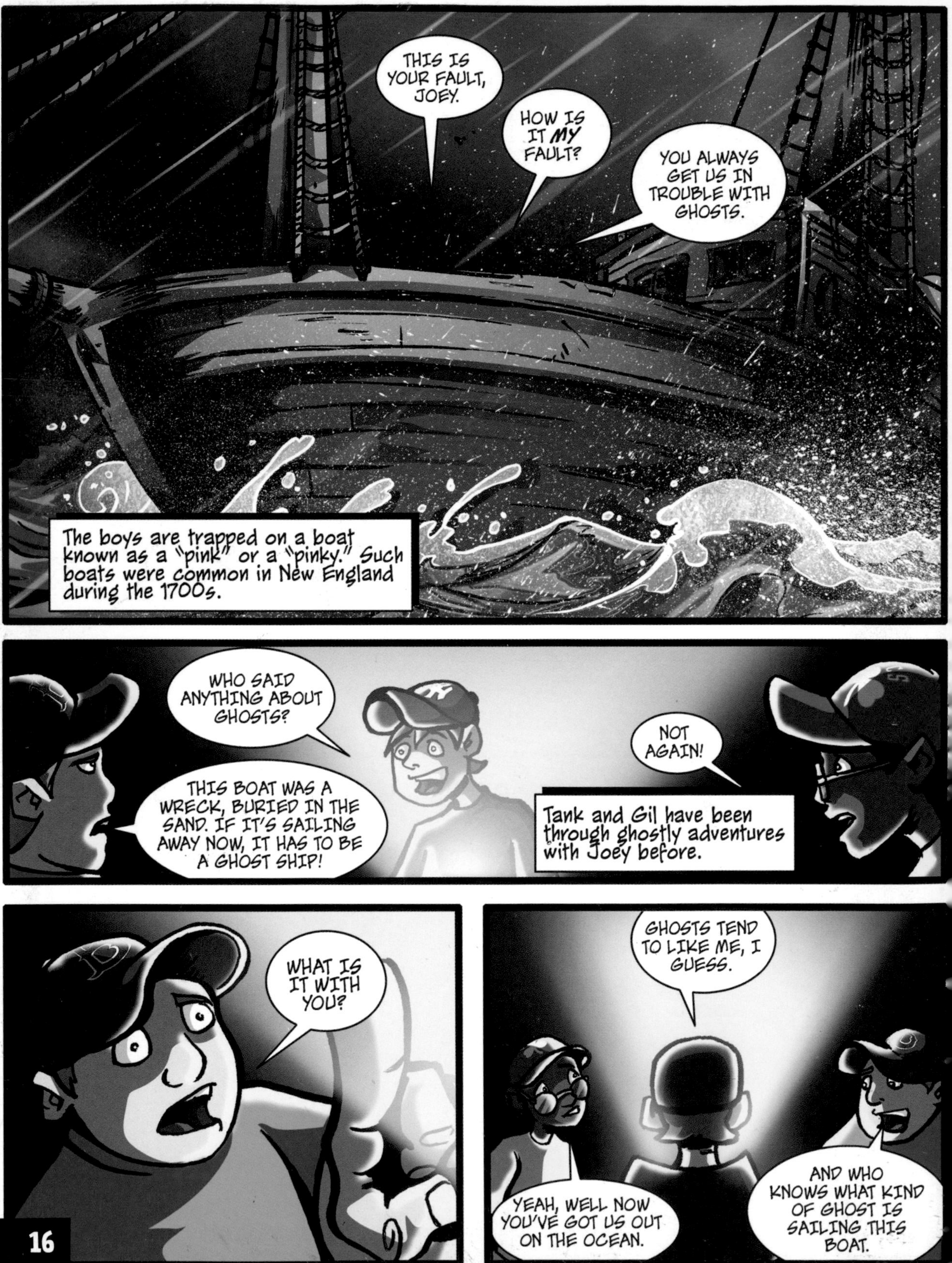
THIS IS YOUR FAULT, JOEY.
HOW IS IT *MY* FAULT?
YOU ALWAYS GET US IN TROUBLE WITH GHOSTS.
The boys are trapped on a boat known as a "pink" or a "pinky." Such boats were common in New England during the 1700s.
WHO SAID ANYTHING ABOUT GHOSTS?
THIS BOAT WAS A WRECK, BURIED IN THE SAND. IF IT'S SAILING AWAY NOW, IT HAS TO BE A GHOST SHIP!
NOT AGAIN!
Tank and Gil have been through ghostly adventures with Joey before.
WHAT IS IT WITH YOU?
GHOSTS TEND TO LIKE ME, I GUESS.
YEAH, WELL NOW YOU'VE GOT US OUT ON THE OCEAN.
AND WHO KNOWS WHAT KIND OF GHOST IS SAILING THIS BOAT.

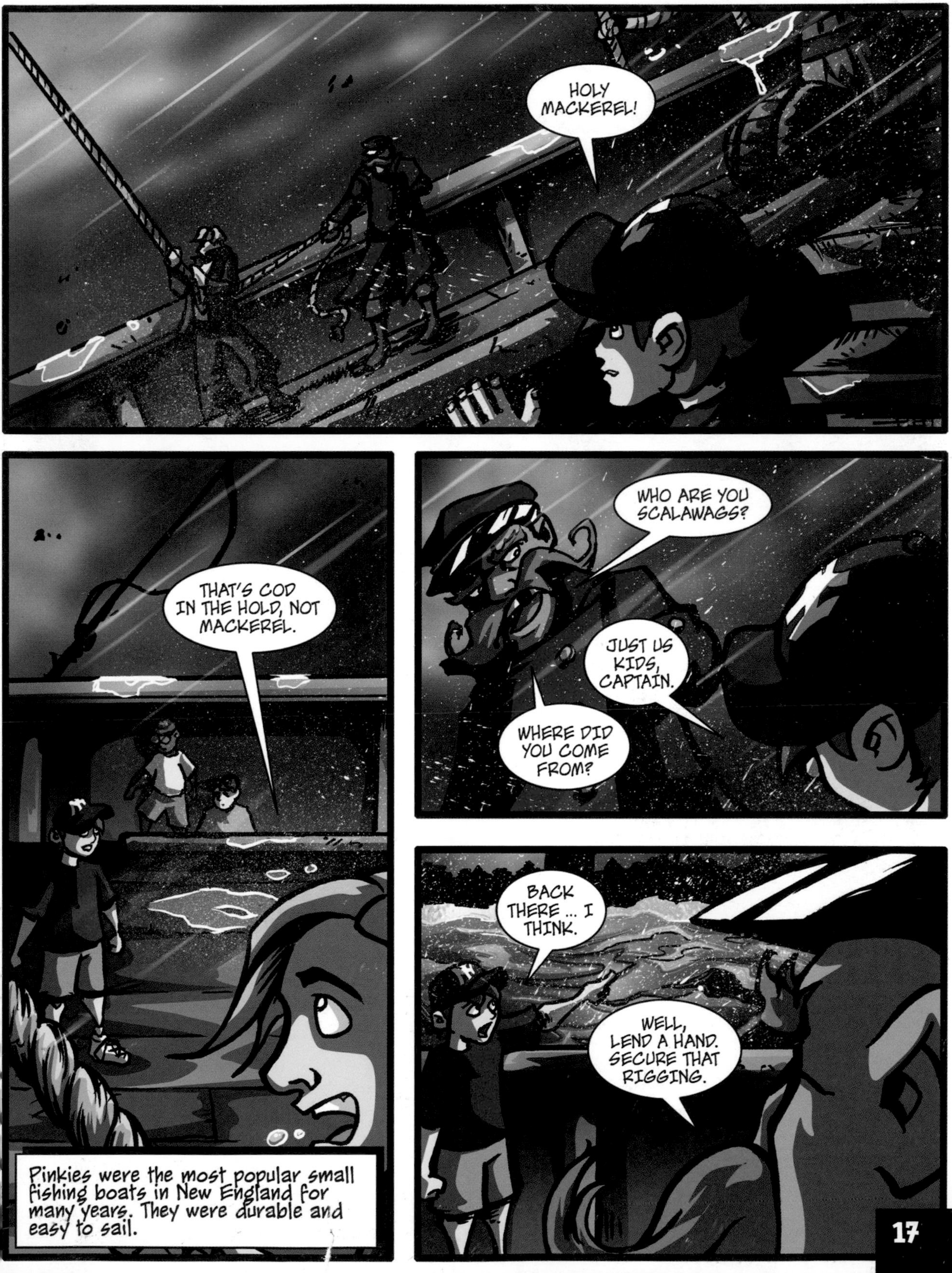
HOLY MACKEREL!
THAT'S COD IN THE HOLD, NOT MACKEREL.
WHO ARE YOU SCALAWAGS?
JUST US KIDS, CAPTAIN.
WHERE DID YOU COME FROM?
BACK THERE ... I THINK.
WELL, LEND A HAND. SECURE THAT RIGGING.
Pinkies were the most popular small fishing boats in New England for many years. They were durable and easy to sail.

THE WHAT?

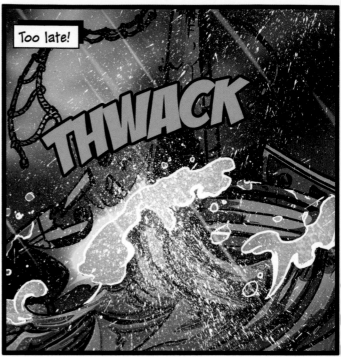

Too late!

THWACK

DROP THE ANCHOR!

THE ANCHOR WON'T HOLD. THE TIDE IS HIGHER THAN I'VE EVER SEEN IN THESE WATERS.

Pinks were easy to steer around the rocky coast, but a storm like this one could swamp even a much larger boat.

HERE COMES ANOTHER ONE!

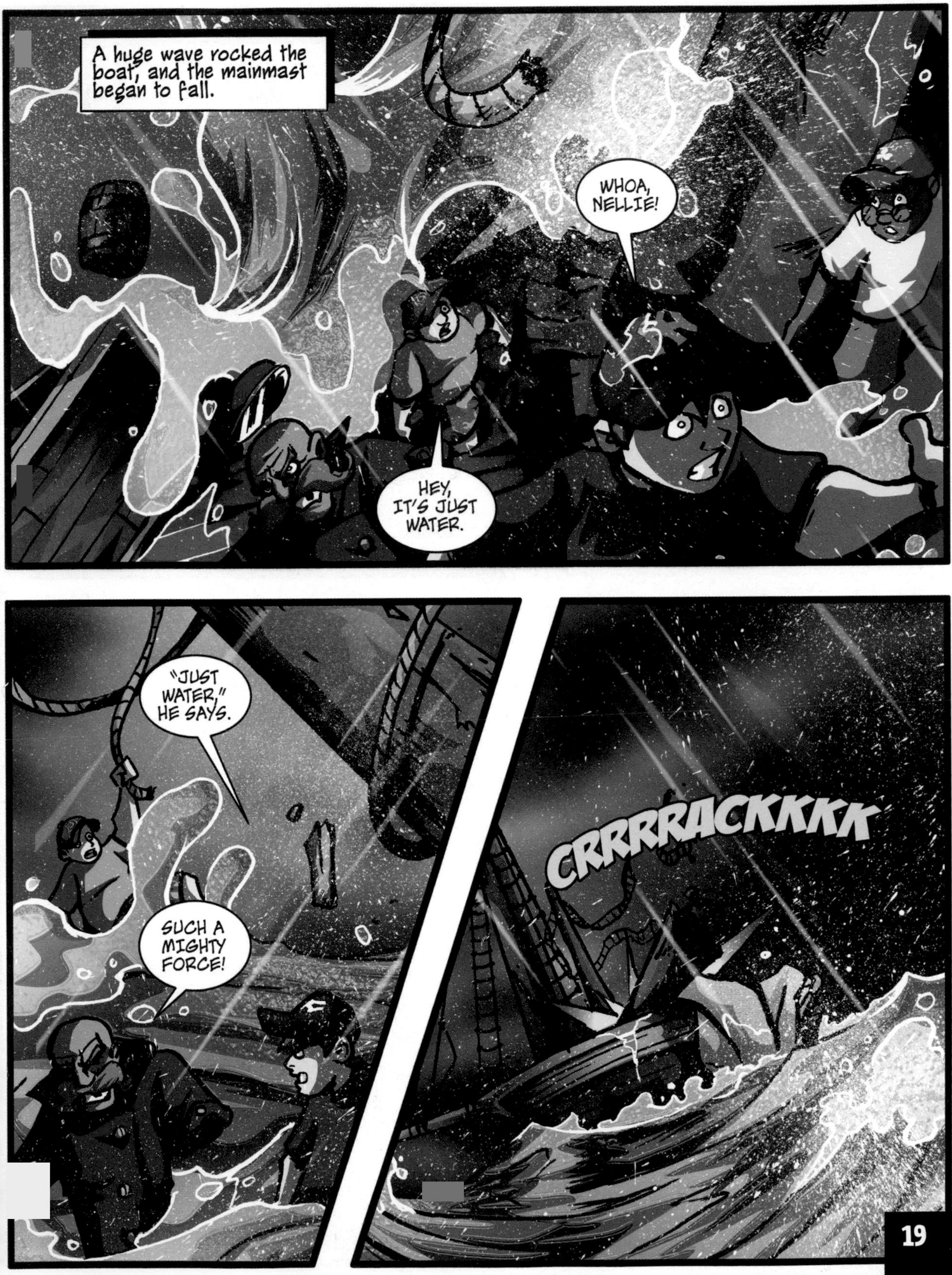
A huge wave rocked the boat, and the mainmast began to fall.
WHOA, NELLIE!
HEY, IT'S JUST WATER.
"JUST WATER," HE SAYS.
SUCH A MIGHTY FORCE!
CRRRRACKKKK

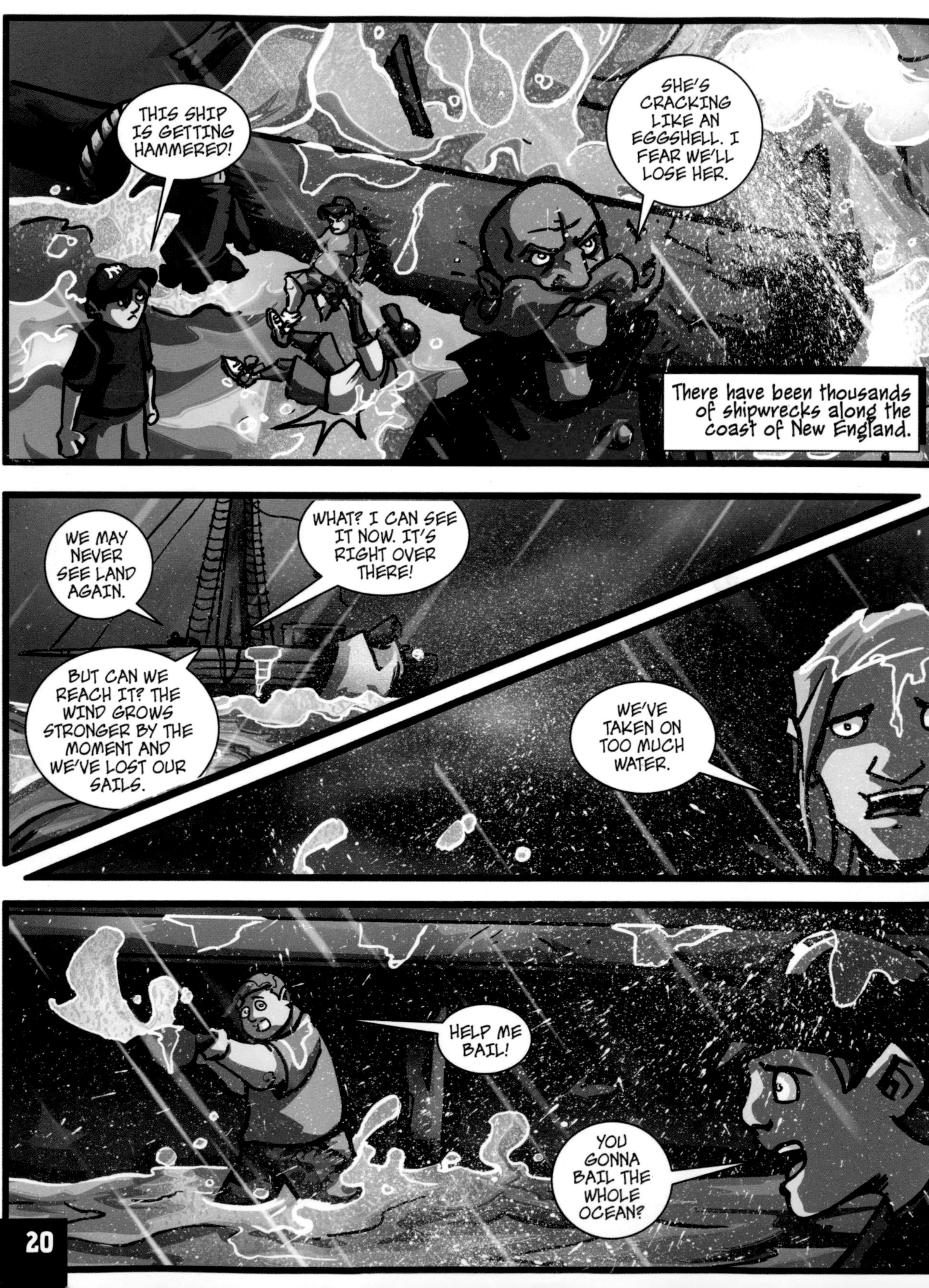
THIS SHIP IS GETTING HAMMERED!
SHE'S CRACKING LIKE AN EGGSHELL. I FEAR WE'LL LOSE HER.
There have been thousands of shipwrecks along the coast of New England.
WE MAY NEVER SEE LAND AGAIN.
WHAT? I CAN SEE IT NOW. IT'S RIGHT OVER THERE!
BUT CAN WE REACH IT? THE WIND GROWS STRONGER BY THE MOMENT AND WE'VE LOST OUR SAILS.
WE'VE TAKEN ON TOO MUCH WATER.
HELP ME BAIL!
YOU GONNA BAIL THE WHOLE OCEAN?

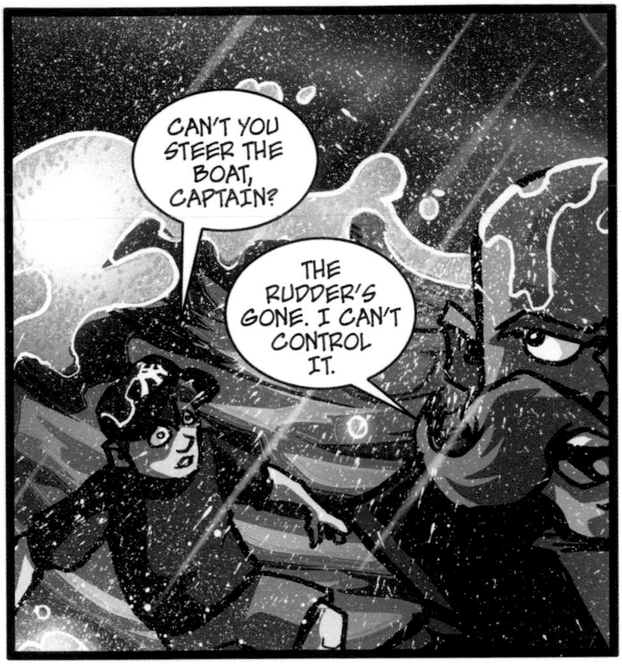
CAN'T YOU STEER THE BOAT, CAPTAIN?
THE RUDDER'S GONE. I CAN'T CONTROL IT.

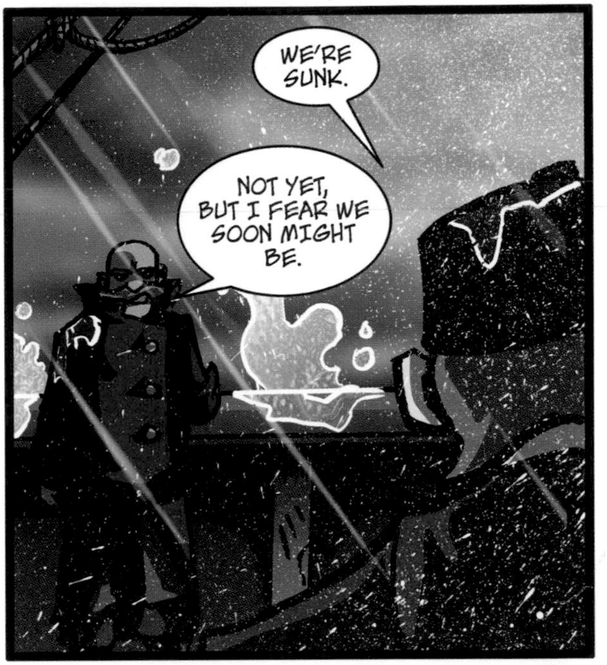
WE'RE SUNK.
NOT YET, BUT I FEAR WE SOON MIGHT BE.

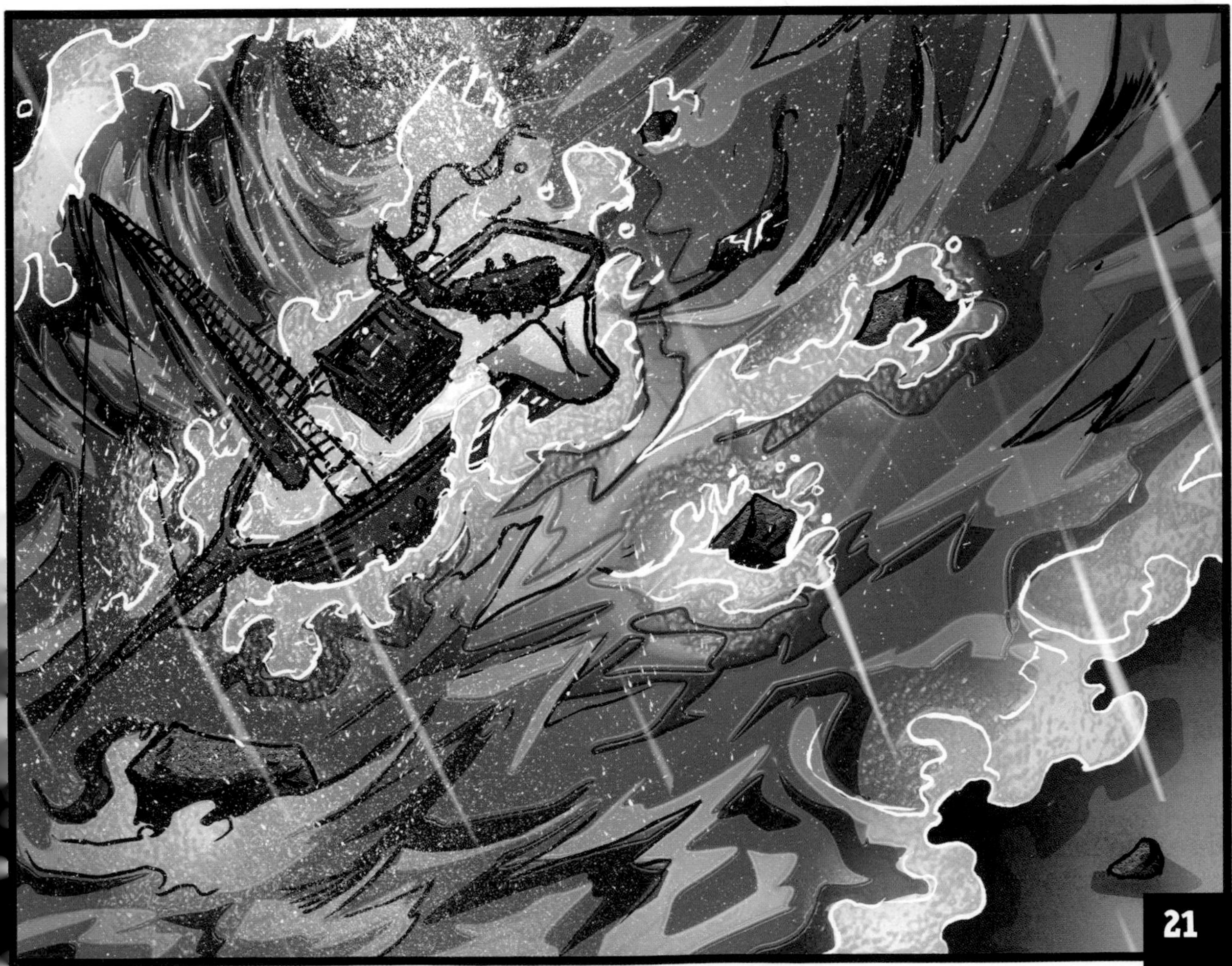

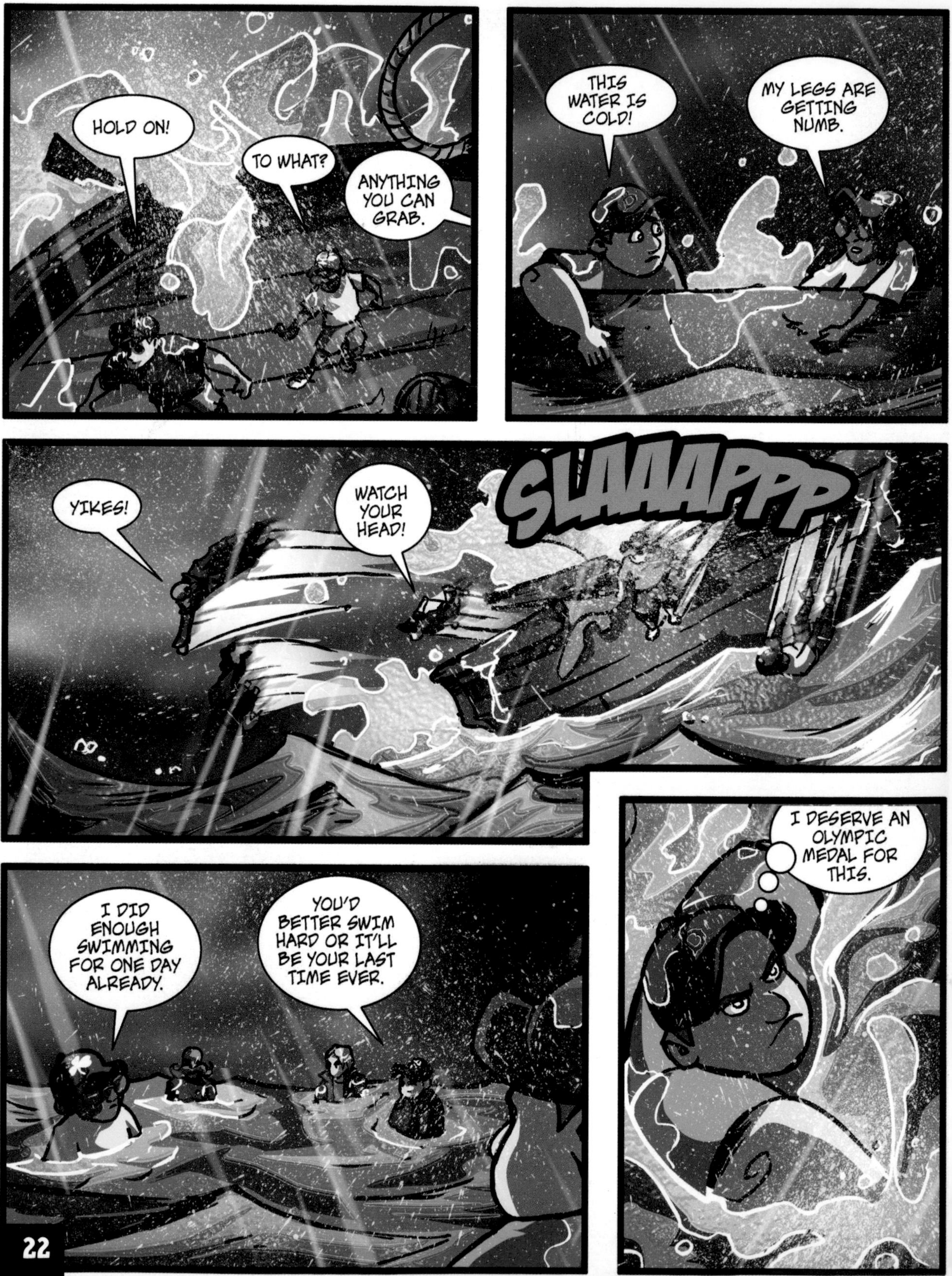
HOLD ON!
TO WHAT?
ANYTHING YOU CAN GRAB.
THIS WATER IS COLD!
MY LEGS ARE GETTING NUMB.
YIKES!
WATCH YOUR HEAD!
SLAAAAPPP
I DESERVE AN OLYMPIC MEDAL FOR THIS.
I DID ENOUGH SWIMMING FOR ONE DAY ALREADY.
YOU'D BETTER SWIM HARD OR IT'LL BE YOUR LAST TIME EVER.

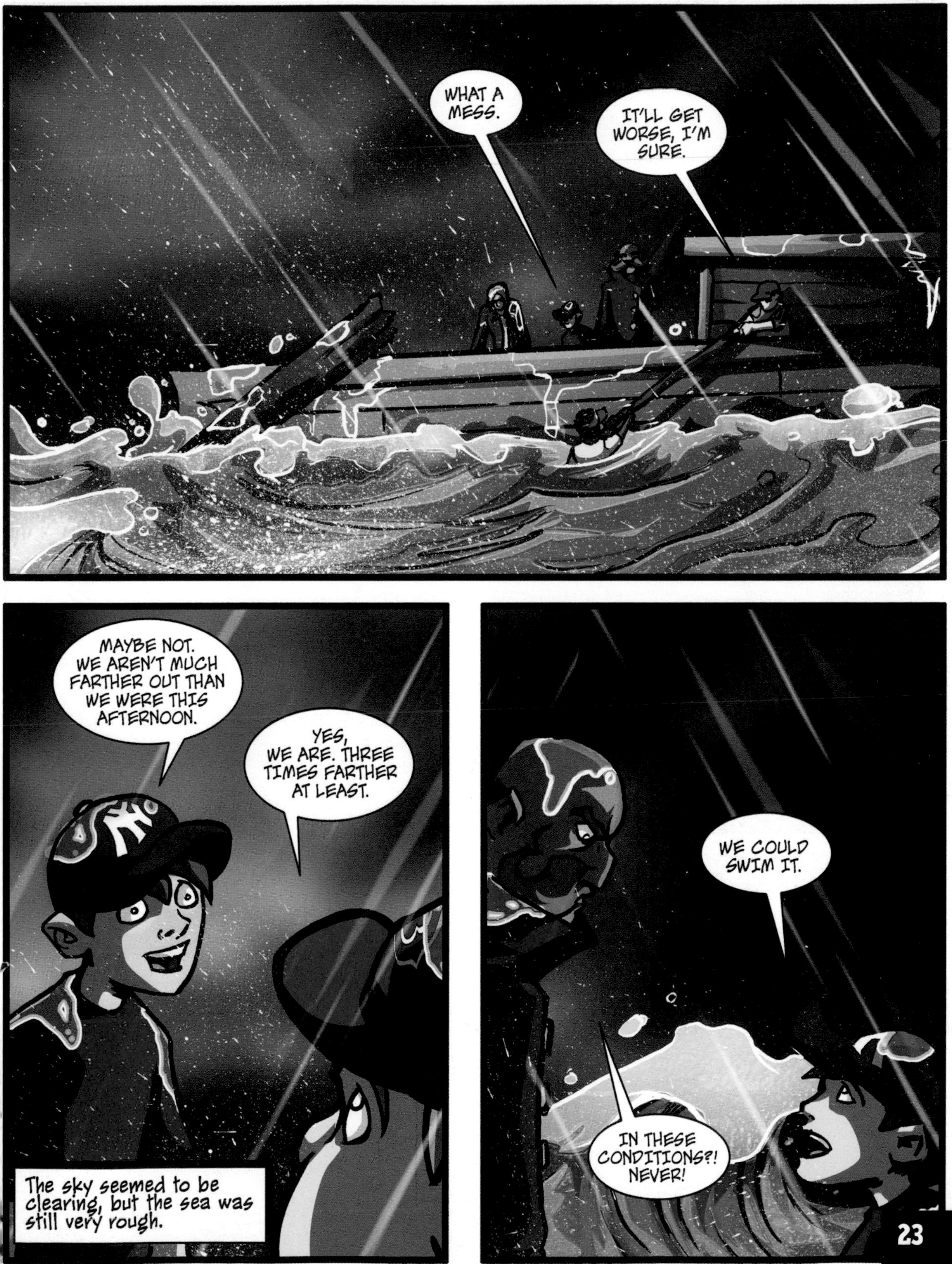
WHAT A MESS.
IT'LL GET WORSE, I'M SURE.
MAYBE NOT. WE AREN'T MUCH FARTHER OUT THAN WE WERE THIS AFTERNOON.
YES, WE ARE. THREE TIMES FARTHER AT LEAST.
The sky seemed to be clearing, but the sea was still very rough.
WE COULD SWIM IT.
IN THESE CONDITIONS?! NEVER!

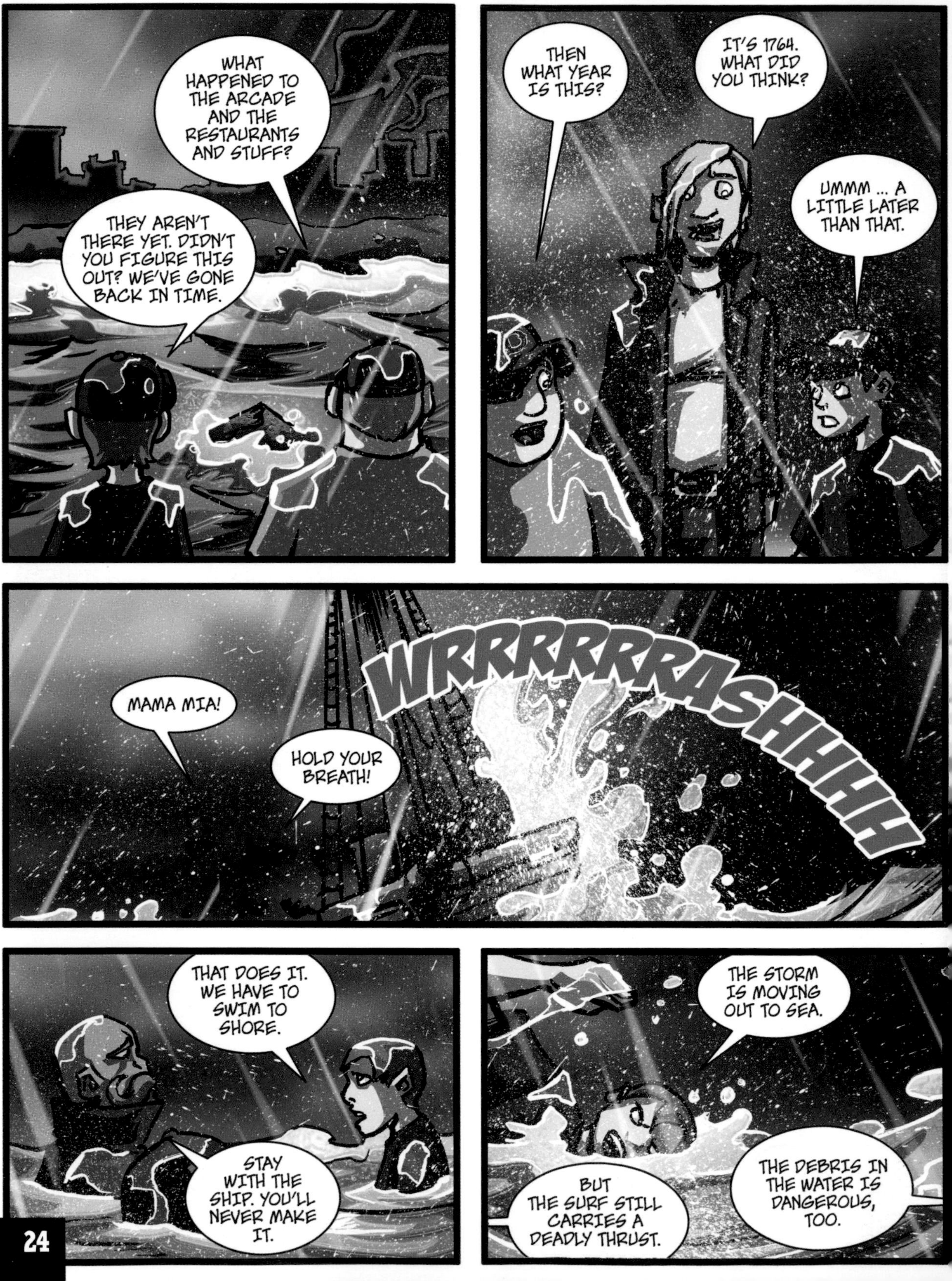
WHAT HAPPENED TO THE ARCADE AND THE RESTAURANTS AND STUFF?
THEY AREN'T THERE YET. DIDN'T YOU FIGURE THIS OUT? WE'VE GONE BACK IN TIME.
THEN WHAT YEAR IS THIS?
IT'S 1764. WHAT DID YOU THINK?
UMMM ... A LITTLE LATER THAN THAT.
WRRRRRRASHHHHH
MAMA MIA!
HOLD YOUR BREATH!
THAT DOES IT. WE HAVE TO SWIM TO SHORE.
STAY WITH THE SHIP. YOU'LL NEVER MAKE IT.
THE STORM IS MOVING OUT TO SEA.
BUT THE SURF STILL CARRIES A DEADLY THRUST.
THE DEBRIS IN THE WATER IS DANGEROUS, TOO.

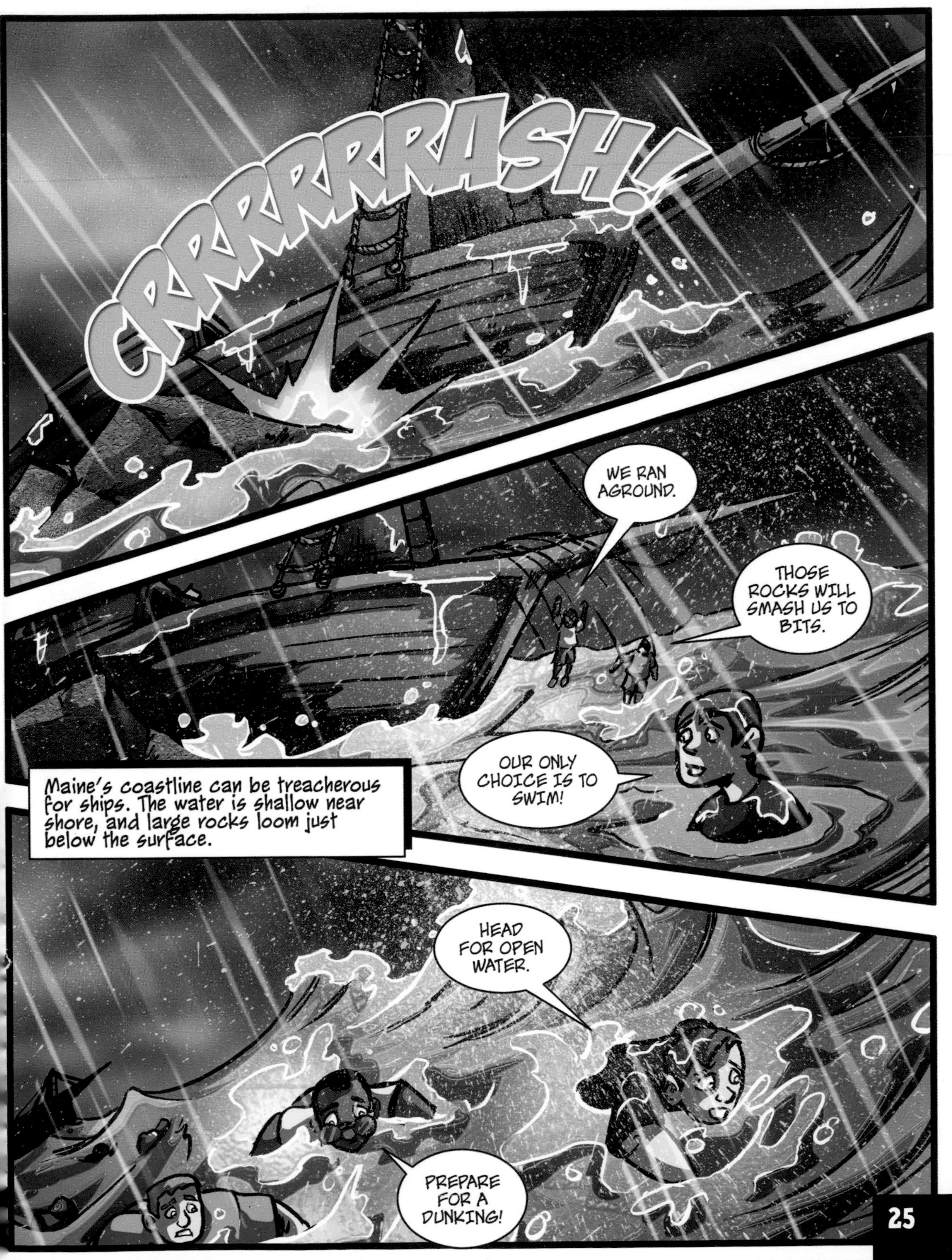
CRRRRRASH!
WE RAN AGROUND.
THOSE ROCKS WILL SMASH US TO BITS.
Maine's coastline can be treacherous for ships. The water is shallow near shore, and large rocks loom just below the surface.
OUR ONLY CHOICE IS TO SWIM!
HEAD FOR OPEN WATER.
PREPARE FOR A DUNKING!

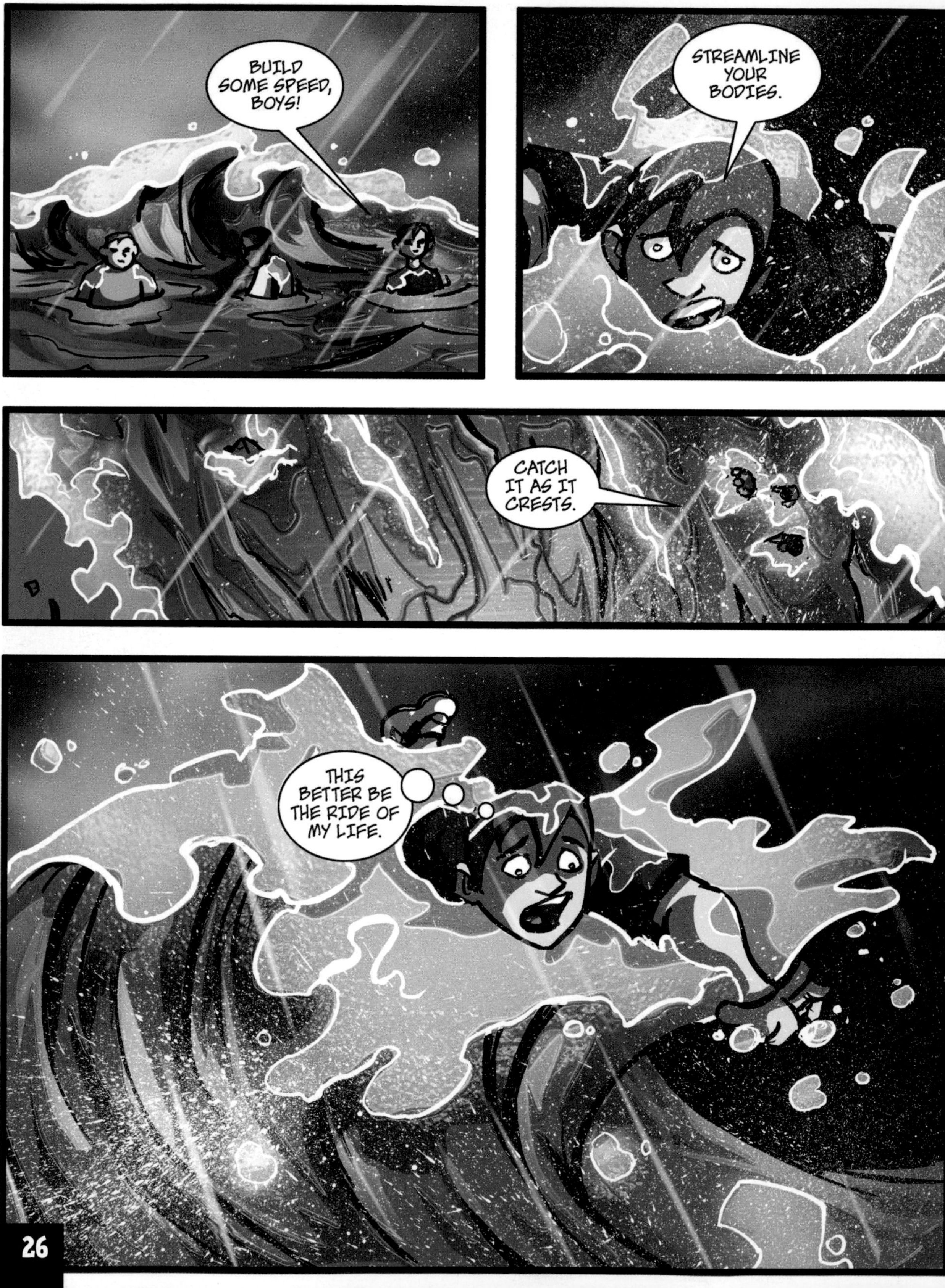
BUILD SOME SPEED, BOYS!
STREAMLINE YOUR BODIES.
CATCH IT AS IT CRESTS.
THIS BETTER BE THE RIDE OF MY LIFE.

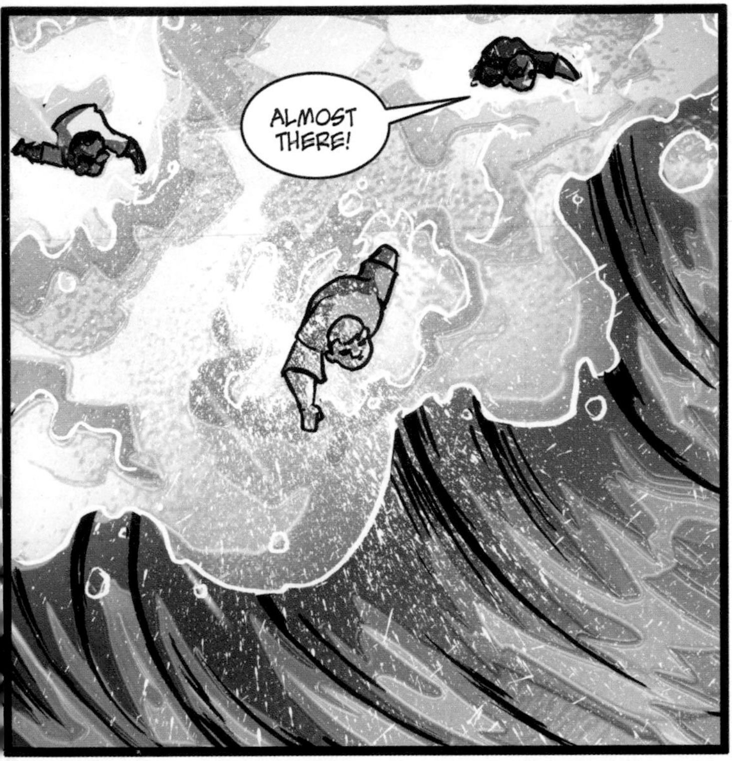
ALMOST THERE!

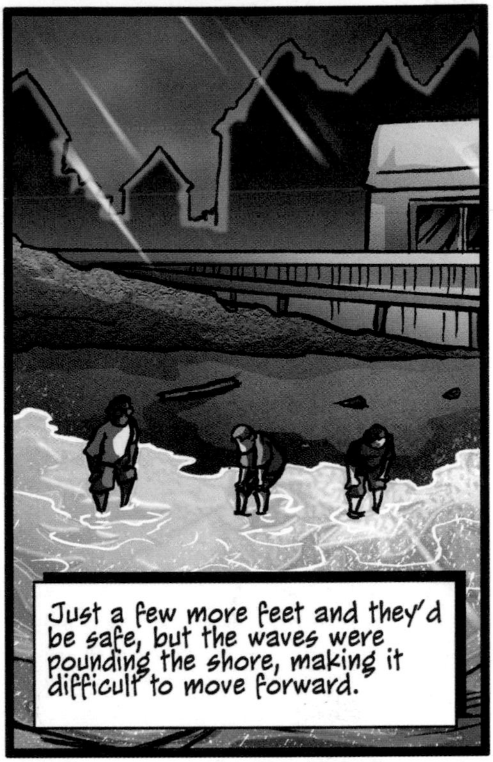
Just a few more feet and they'd be safe, but the waves were pounding the shore, making it difficult to move forward.

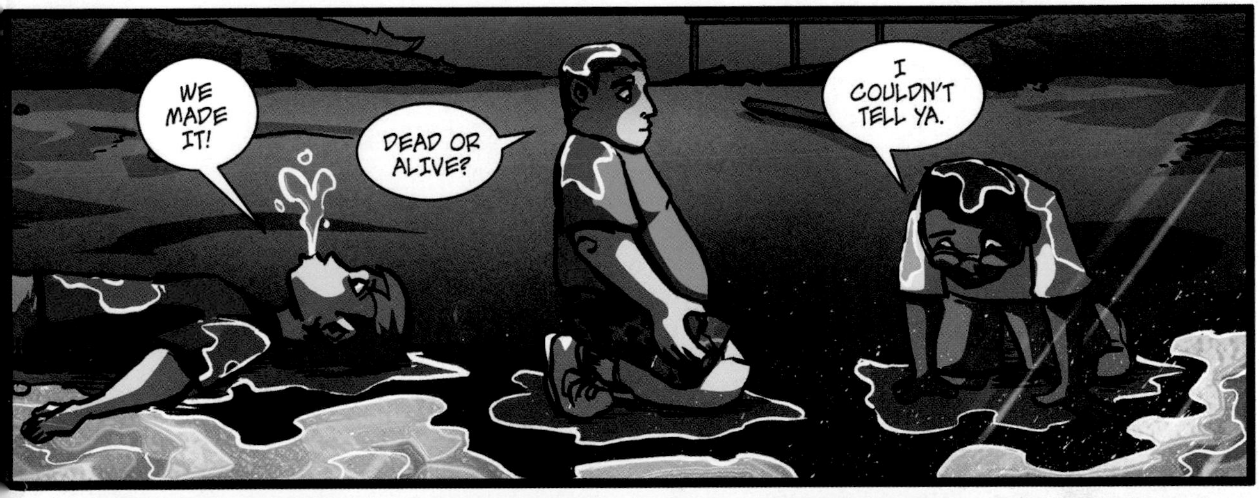
WE MADE IT!
DEAD OR ALIVE?
I COULDN'T TELL YA.

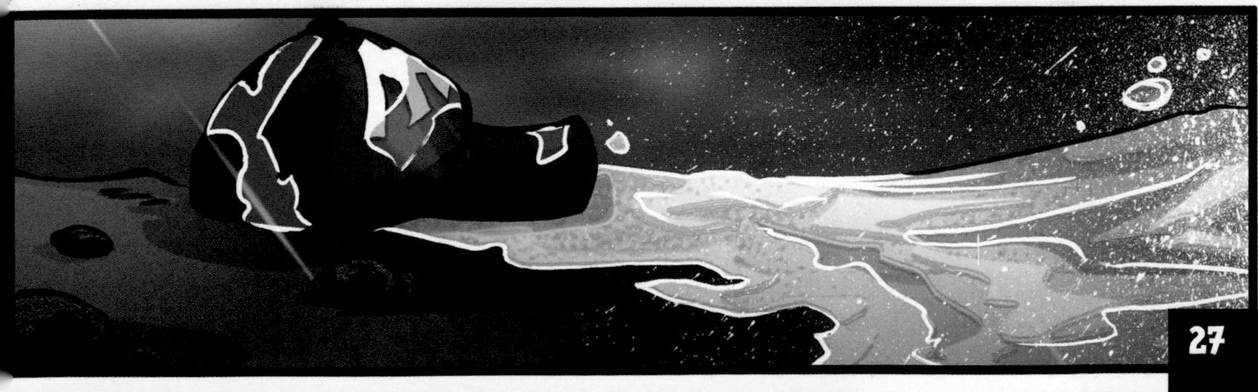

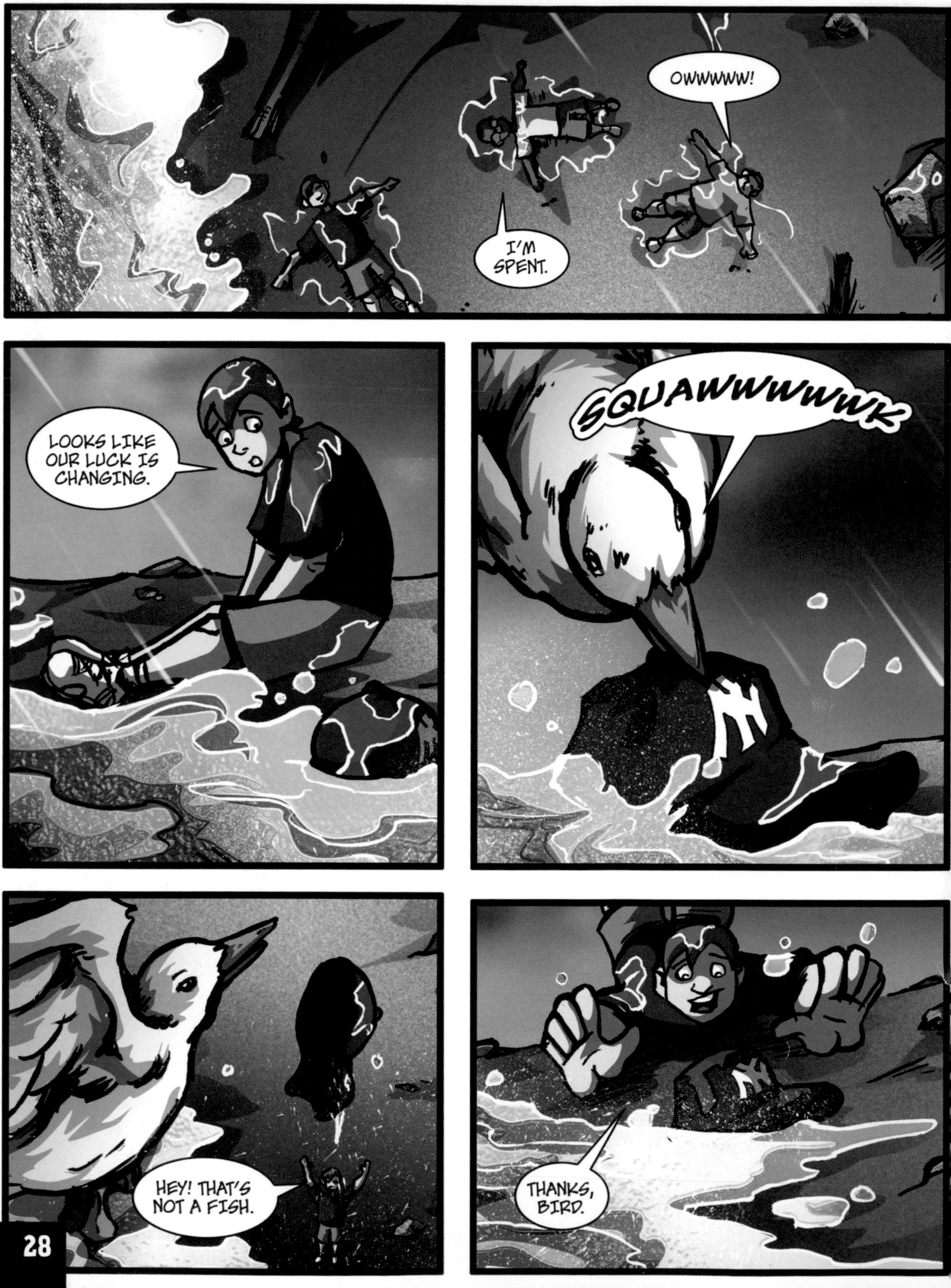
OWWWWW!
I'M SPENT.
LOOKS LIKE OUR LUCK IS CHANGING.
SQUAWWWWWWK
HEY! THAT'S NOT A FISH.
THANKS, BIRD.

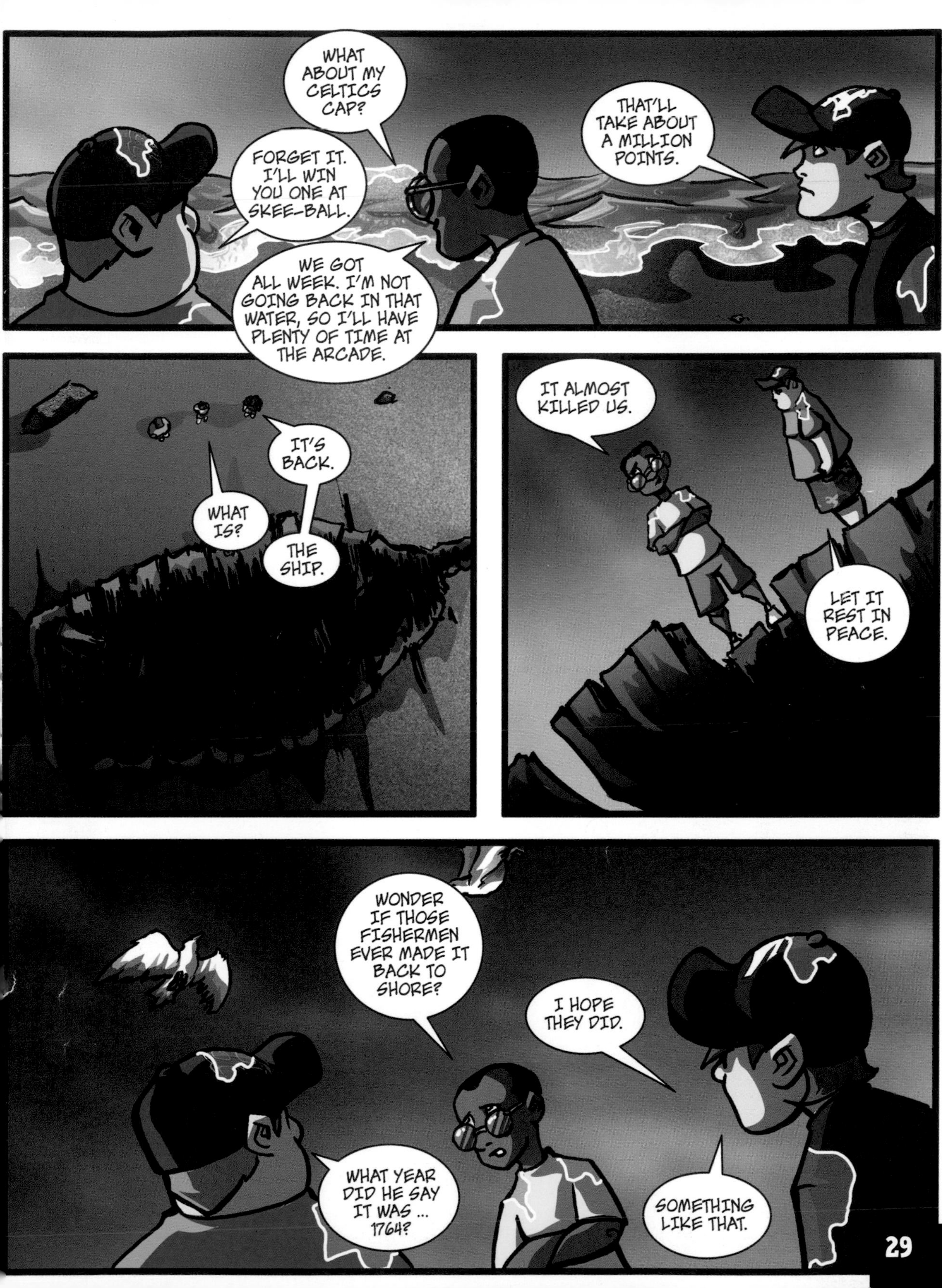
WHAT ABOUT MY CELTICS CAP?
FORGET IT. I'LL WIN YOU ONE AT SKEE-BALL.
THAT'LL TAKE ABOUT A MILLION POINTS.
WE GOT ALL WEEK. I'M NOT GOING BACK IN THAT WATER, SO I'LL HAVE PLENTY OF TIME AT THE ARCADE.
IT'S BACK.
WHAT IS?
THE SHIP.
IT ALMOST KILLED US.
LET IT REST IN PEACE.
WONDER IF THOSE FISHERMEN EVER MADE IT BACK TO SHORE?
I HOPE THEY DID.
WHAT YEAR DID HE SAY IT WAS ... 1764?
SOMETHING LIKE THAT.

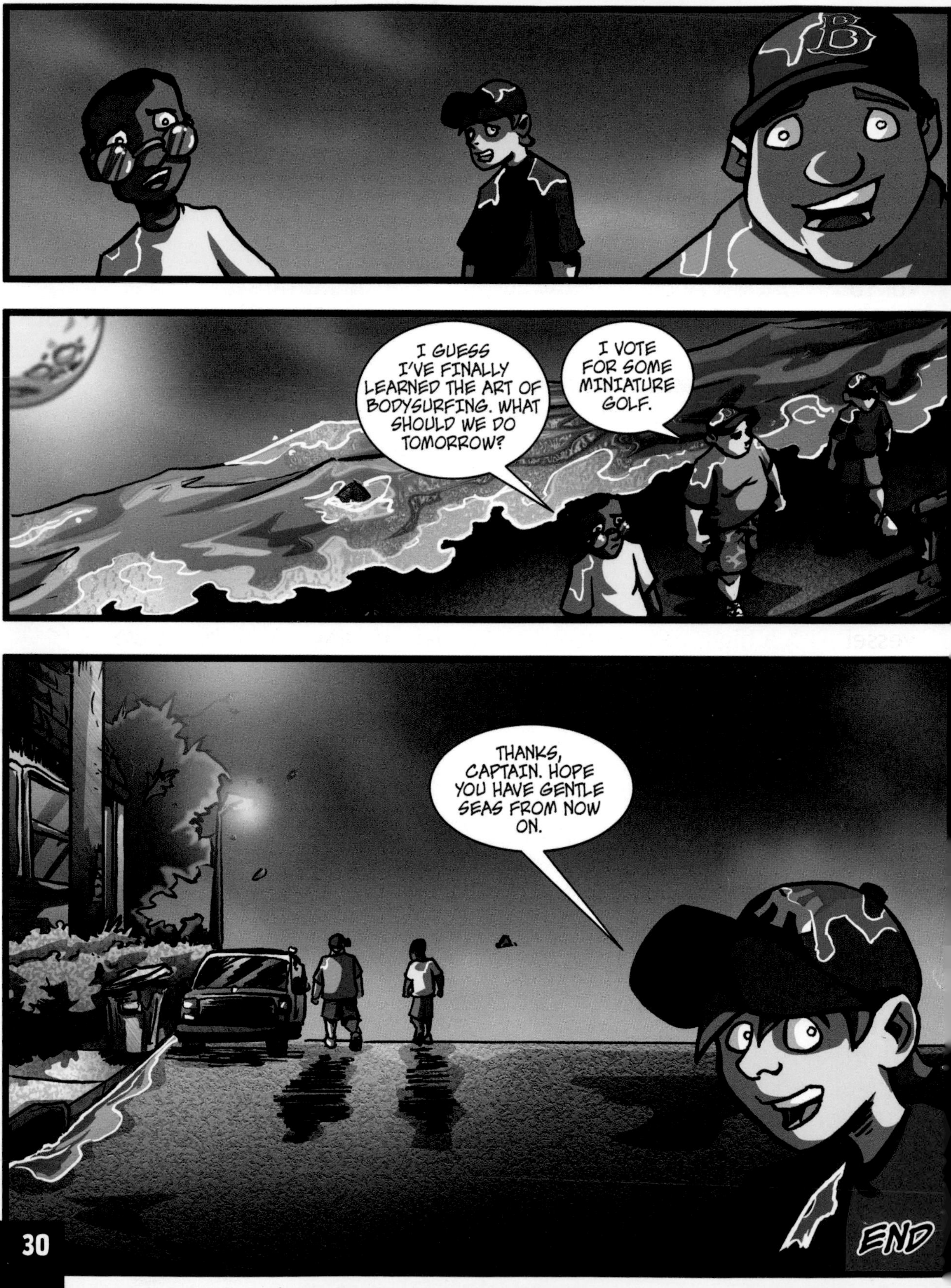
I GUESS I'VE FINALLY LEARNED THE ART OF BODYSURFING. WHAT SHOULD WE DO TOMORROW?
I VOTE FOR SOME MINIATURE GOLF.
THANKS, CAPTAIN. HOPE YOU HAVE GENTLE SEAS FROM NOW ON.
END

# THE SHORT SANDS SHIPWRECK

Short Sands Beach in York, Maine, is usually a peaceful place where residents walk their dogs, tourists splash in the ocean, and seagulls hunt for food. But every once in a while, a powerful storm will uncover an interesting bit of New England's past.

Town officials believe that there have been more than 60 shipwrecks in York over the past few centuries. The wreck of a 250-year-old ship is buried beneath the Short Sands Beach. Not much is known about the ship, but the high tides and rough surf of an April storm can sweep several feet of sand from the beach. One year, the tides left the frame of the ship exposed.

Historians determined that the ship was probably a "pinky," a vessel with a high, narrow stern and square rigging. Such boats were popular in Maine because they were easy to maneuver along the state's rocky coastline. They were used for fishing and for hauling cargo during the 1700s. The ship buried at Short Sands Beach is believed to be from around the time of the Revolutionary War (1775-1783).

Storms uncover the ship every 20 or 30 years or so, and town officials cover it with sand again to help preserve it. The ship has been recorded as an archaeological site by the Historical Preservation Commission. It will be studied in detail at some future date.

Short Sands Beach is a popular destination for ocean lovers. Just yards from the beach is a charming main street with an arcade. There are many restaurants where tourists can enjoy saltwater taffy, fresh fish and lobsters, ice cream, and other great food.

# GLOSSARY

**aground** - on the land or shore.

**crest** - the top of a wave.

**debris** - the remains of something broken or destroyed.

**decade** - a period of ten years.

**durable** - able to exist for a long time without weakening.

**rigging** - the ropes and chains used to work a ship's sails.

**rudder** - a movable arm on a ship attached at the rear end.  The rudder controls the forward movement of a ship.

**scalawag** - rascal.

**streamlined** - designed to reduce drag or resistance to motion when moving through air or water.

**treacherous** - having hidden dangers.

# WEB SITES

To learn more about the Short Sands shipwreck, visit ABDO Group online at **www.abdopublishing.com**.  Web sites about the Short Sands shipwreck are featured on our Book Links page.  These links are routinely monitored and updated to provide the most current information available.